MW00614083

# Audrey's Disappearance

## Jenifer Parent

Copyright © 2021 Jenifer Parent

All rights reserved.
No part of this book may be reproduced or used in
any manner without written permission of the copyright
owner except for the use of quotations in a book review.

This is a work of fiction. Names, characters,
organizations, places, events, and incidents are either
the product of the author's imagination or are used
fictitiously. Any resemblance to actual people, living
or dead, or to businesses, companies, events,
institutions, or locales is entirely coincidental.

First paperback edition April 2021

Book cover design by BetiBup33 Design Studio

ISBN 978-1-7367152-1-5 (paperback)
ISBN 978-1-7367152-0-8 (ebook)

*Audrey's Disappearance* is the first book in
The Detective Harris Series.

JeniferParentAuthor.com

*Also by Jenifer Parent*

**The Detective Harris Series**
*A Twin's Fate*
*Always a Killer Nearby*

*For Dennis, who encourages me to take risks and follow my dreams*

# Prologue

Detective Darryl Harris slowly drove past the red and blue flashing lights of the police cars parked along the beach ramp on the south end of Cocoa Beach. Having found the last available parking space, he slid out of his smoke-gray Dodge Charger. The homicide detective hastened toward the officer standing guard near the crime scene investigation (CSI) van at the end of the ramp.

Glancing down at his watch, Darryl noted the time: 3:37. It was nearly freezing outside at 35 degrees—colder than usual for Florida, even at this time of morning in January. Darryl's hands were balled into fists in his jacket pockets to warm them. A badge sat on his right hip, a 9mm gun on his left.

"Officer Kentz, what do we know so far about the victim?"

Officer William Kentz looked up from his cell phone and smirked. "Detective, nice haircut. You look just like a young Denzel Washington."

Not in the mood for compliments, Darryl gave him a polite smile and replied, "Thanks. And the victim?"

"Of course. I was the first to arrive to the scene when the call came in. The victim appears to be young—no older than her teens. The CSI is processing the body now."

"Thanks," Darryl said, taking off for the beach. As he stepped off the asphalt onto the sand, he stopped momentarily to scan the coastline covered in a swarm of officers and their K9s. Catching sight of the bright beam of light coming from the spotlight approximately thirty yards away, Darryl veered right toward the reason for all the commotion.

With high tide only a couple of hours away, there was an urgency to search the surrounding area before the ocean waves washed away any evidence. Even more crucial was the job of the CSI who was searching the body for DNA or other clues before being transported to the Brevard County Medical Examiner's Office.

The victim, a young woman who had been stabbed to death and discarded on the beach, was found by the local beach patrol when they were doing their nightly rounds up the six-mile stretch of beach in the small town of Cocoa Beach.

Darryl took the most direct path toward the CSI, while steering clear of the cops and their dogs. It was not a simple task to walk in the sand with heavy Oxford boots on, but he was determined to get a glimpse at the latest victim.

He had been investigating a series of kidnappings and murders in the area for quite some time. Therefore, it didn't surprise Darryl when, half an hour ago, he was awakened by a phone call asking him to come down to the beach to verify if the most recent victim had the same marking as the others who fell prey to his serial killer. A psychopath referred to as the "Cocoa Beach Killer" by the local news media.

A certain horrific detail of the prior murders hadn't been released to the public, so the police could distinguish between the real killer and any potential copycats. The young women had been so severely mistreated—starved, sexually assaulted, and tortured—only their faces were uncovered when the medical examiner got a positive ID from family members.

"Detective Harris, sorry to call you in the middle of the night. I thought you may be interested in seeing the body right away. And I remembered Captain Reynolds was still on a cruise with his wife," CSI Melanie Crosby said, having just zipped the body bag. Slowly rising from her kneeling position, she got to her feet to stand next to the detective.

He couldn't help noticing how attractive Mel was, even at this time of night. Her blue jeans and black jacket were well-fitted to her slim body. She wore her long dark hair up in a high ponytail, which was being blown in all directions by the breeze off the ocean. The look gave her the appearance of someone much younger than thirty.

Having worked with her on many cases, Darryl was well acquainted with Mel—in more ways than one. The night they spent together a month ago had been a rebound for him, or more of a lapse in judgement.

To his surprise, Mel had never brought up what happened between them that night, or more importantly, the fact that Darryl had left before she woke.

Every time their paths crossed, he expected her to be angry with him or to question why he left without saying a word. Maybe it would've made him feel better if she had.

"You were right to call me. What have you found so far?" At this point, he quickly glanced down at the body bag.

Mel, who knew Darryl desperately needed a lead in his investigation, got back down on her knees.

As she unzipped the body bag, Darryl instantly noticed the far-off look in the victim's frozen stare. Then the hollowed cheeks that confirmed her malnourishment. If that wasn't evidence enough of the serial killer's MO, the detective's pulse quickened at the sight of the final detail—the word *SLUT* sliced into the victim's abdomen.

The naked girl had unmistakably been tortured and stabbed by the same murderer he was looking for. *The bastard did it again!* he shouted inwardly.

She was the seventh girl in less than four years to be discovered in this state. All of the victims' abused bodies were found unclothed and discarded on the beach.

There was no doubt, based on the nature of the teenager's injuries, the same deviant was responsible for her death. *I need to find this guy before another young woman faces the same horrendous fate.*

# Chapter 1

*August 2017*

A blast of cold air blew across her face, and the change in temperature brought her to consciousness. She came to with a throbbing headache. Her eyes struggled to see through the darkness, and a strong musty smell brought a wave of nausea.

Suddenly, Audrey realized what little she could see didn't look familiar. *Where am I?! This isn't my room!* She sat up as panic took hold. *This can't be happening!* Her heart was pounding. She frantically scanned the room for anything that would tell her where she was, but it was too dark. Closing her eyes, she took a deep breath to steady her nerves. *I can't lose it now. There's too much at stake.*

Finally opening her eyes, she realized she was wearing the clothes she had on that morning. *Is it still Friday? How long have I been unconscious?* She couldn't tell what time of day it was and brushed her hands along the mattress hoping to find her cell phone or anything else she previously had with her. But her search was useless; there was only a pillow and fitted sheet on the mattress with her.

Praying she could hear something—anything—that'd give her a clue to where she was, Audrey closed her eyes again and listened for familiar sounds. For all she knew she was in a stranger's house, or an abandoned building, or possibly a secluded location in the middle of nowhere.

Her stomach did nervous flips. It was possible she was completely alone. Or worse, she wasn't. Tears threatened to fall.

Since the headache and nausea had worsened when she sat up, Audrey rested her head on the pillow and thought back to her last memory before waking up in this strange room.

***

Around ten o'clock Friday morning, Audrey and her best friend, Natalie Anderson, had met up to go surfing at their favorite spot in their hometown of Cocoa Beach, Florida.

Audrey had the day off from her job as a lifeguard at the Mirage Beach Resort, and Natalie didn't have to be at her hostess job at a local high-end Italian restaurant until seven that evening.

The best friends hadn't seen much of each other over the past month. While they each had been faced with challenging news, neither entrusted the other with what they were going through.

Instead, in between riding the waves on their surfboards, Audrey and Natalie chatted about the latest celebrity news, books they were reading, and pretty much anything outside of the real issues they were facing.

"I haven't seen much of you lately, not since the Fourth of July party. Is everything okay with you?" Natalie asked as they took a break to sit on their boards with their legs dangling in the cool ocean water.

Audrey wasn't surprised by her friend's question. No matter how much she tried to act like her usual self, she had too much on her mind. Natalie had already caught her emerald green eyes staring into space several times that morning.

"Yeah, I've just been thinking about my move to Gainesville in a couple of weeks, along with starting college and leaving behind my family and friends. It seems overwhelming at times," Audrey admitted with a small smile, hoping that'd be enough of an explanation for now. There were crucial decisions to make, and her future was going to significantly change no matter what she decided. Her life had been completely planned out prior to summer starting, but now all those plans were dashed to pieces.

Sweeping her long dark brown hair off her shoulders, Audrey said, "Speaking of which, you haven't exactly been yourself lately. Anything bothering *you*?" Audrey countered, not only because she was truly concerned, but also to move the topic of conversation away from her. It was possible Natalie was still brokenhearted from her breakup with Carl.

"No. Same as you. College starting soon and all." Natalie gave her a smile that didn't quite make it to her icy blue eyes.

It didn't sound like the whole truth, but who was Audrey to point it out? Especially since she was holding back a secret of her own.

"Well, let's make it a goal to stay in touch, even when we're living hundreds of miles from each other. I need you in my life." Audrey bit the inside of her cheek to hold back her emotions.

Natalie looked over at her with a genuine smile that caused her dimples to deepen. "I know. I need you too."

To lighten the mood, Audrey dipped her hand into the ocean and splashed Natalie's golden blonde hair with a handful of salty water. When Natalie reciprocated, Audrey found herself enjoying the refreshing feel of the cool water on her warm skin.

An hour later, the waves started dying down. Sloshing through the saltwater, the teenagers carried their surfboards to shore to pack up their stuff.

Audrey pulled her cell phone out of her beach bag. "It's already past one! I can't believe how fast time goes now that we've graduated high school. I better get ready for dinner with Keith. He's picking me up at five, and I have to run an errand on the way home."

Since Audrey and Keith hadn't seen each other for over a month, she didn't want to be late. She dried off, threw her denim shorts and blue tank top on over her black one-piece bathing suit, then slipped on her flip flops.

Once she had gathered her belongings, she gave Natalie a hug good-bye and promised to call her later that evening to make plans for the weekend.

It wasn't unusual for Audrey to leave the beach before her friend, since she normally had to run off to volleyball practice or go to work earlier than Natalie. With her beach bag slung over one shoulder and her surfboard nestled under her other arm, Audrey strolled back to her car, which was parked at the Methodist Church up the street.

\*\*\*

Now, sitting on the mattress in the dark with her arms crossed as she rubbed her upper arms, Audrey struggled to remember what happened when she got to the church parking lot.

Then it all came back in a flash! She remembered crossing the street and walking around the corner of the church where the parking lot was. Opening her beach bag to search for her car keys, she heard someone move behind her. Before she could turn around, the person had taken hold of her with one large hand around her mouth and the other around her torso. Her surfboard hit the ground, while the items in her beach bag spilled out at her feet when the bag fell from her shoulder.

The man wasn't much taller than her, but he was much stronger. When Audrey was about to use the self-defense moves she had learned less than a year ago, she felt a sharp jab in her neck. Her vision instantly went hazy, then black.

In the darkness, Audrey anxiously felt around her neck and found the area where she had experienced the painful jab. *It was a needle!* She must've been drugged with something. It explained why she didn't remember being brought to this place. *But who did this?! And why me?!*

More terrifying was the question of what her captor wanted from her. Audrey's parents were well off, but not rich. If the kidnapper was expecting to be paid a large ransom, then Audrey was in serious trouble.

*I need to get out of this room. And I need to find something to protect myself in case someone is planning to come back and hurt me.*

The cold air she felt earlier was coming from above the mattress. *Must be an air vent.* Audrey set her feet on the ground, feeling the cool concrete slab. She barely made out her Adidas flip flops by the mattress. She slipped them on and pushed herself up off the mattress. But it was more of an effort than she expected; she began to sway and caught her balance just in time to not fall back.

With cautious footing, she reached the nearest wall—also concrete block. The absence of drywall made the space feel more like a prison than a room. She shook off the thought. Hugging the wall as she crept along, she stopped at a corner a few yards from the mattress and moved her hands up and down the walls in search of a light switch.

If there were any windows in the room, they must be boarded up. This wasn't uncommon during hurricane season, but it hadn't been an active year for hurricanes in Florida. Then it dawned on her: *I might not be in Florida anymore.* But that was another thought she couldn't dwell on right now.

Audrey passed the second corner and felt a break in the wall indicating a door. Eagerly, she searched for the doorknob. She turned and pulled on the knob, but the door was locked from the other side.

The disappointment was devastating. She instantly got choked up. Leaning her forehead against the door, she fought to hold back fresh tears.

After a long moment, she lifted her head and continued creeping alongside the walls until she nearly knocked over a five-gallon bucket that was sitting in the third corner of the room.

Audrey cautiously looked inside, but it was too dark to see if anything was in it. She lifted it. Empty. *Why is it here?* She looked behind the bucket and saw a roll of toilet paper. *Was it left for me to use as a toilet?*

Shivers ran down her arms and her nausea intensified. How long was she supposed to stay in this room? *None of this makes sense!*

A foot away from the bucket, she came across a single bottle of water sitting on the floor. She decided against drinking from it, even though she felt nauseous and extremely dehydrated.

Back at the mattress, she decided that her only option of escaping was through the air vent above her. She shuffled back over to the bucket and carried it to the mattress where she set it upside down. While bracing one hand on the wall for support, she carefully got on top of the bucket and reached up with her other hand as far as she could. Sadly, the ceiling was still far too high for her to get to the air vent.

After putting the bucket back in the corner, she slumped back down on the mattress. Since she didn't find a way out of the room or anything that would tell her where she was, she felt as hopeless as she did when she woke up.

There was too much riding on her getting out of this room. And while she knew she needed to be strong for whatever was going to happen to her here, she finally allowed herself to give in to the emotions that had been threatening to engulf her. She sobbed into the pillow.

# Chapter 2

When Audrey had left the beach to get ready for her dinner date with Keith, Natalie had decided to stay and surf.

Nearly a month ago, she and Carl Bennett had broken up. Since then, Natalie had been spending most of her time alone—either at the beach or at home reading books or catching up on her favorite sitcoms. In a couple of weeks, she'd be attending Stetson University in Deland, majoring in business management.

She and Audrey had been best friends since kindergarten. Since neither of them had siblings, they spent a lot of time at each other's houses on the weekends and during summer breaks. They had a lot in common, outside of their physical differences.

Audrey was five feet ten inches tall and very lean. Since she had braces and tackled stubborn acne in middle school, by the time she started as a freshman at Cocoa Beach High School she was model material.

Natalie, in contrast, was five feet four inches tall and curvier than her friend. She wasn't overweight, but she also wasn't slim in comparison to her best friend. And while Natalie wasn't athletic compared to Audrey, she did enjoy surfing and swimming in the ocean.

Now that Natalie was out of the water, she took her time drying off. After slipping on her purple and blue tie-dye coverup and Sketcher flip flops, she gathered her surfboard and other belongings and headed to her white Toyota Corolla in a nearby church parking lot. As was her routine, she had parked next to Audrey's car.

It was a five-minute walk up to the church. Since it was an overcast day, the temperature outside wasn't nearly as intense as it usually was this time of day in Florida in early August. At ninety degrees and eighty percent humidity, it could've been a lot worse.

As Natalie approached the parking lot, she saw Audrey's blue Hyundai Sonata. She walked over to the car expecting to see Audrey talking on her cell phone.

But Audrey wasn't in her car. Or anywhere in sight. Natalie pulled her cell phone out of her beach bag and dialed Audrey's number. The phone rang until it went to voice mail. She hit redial but got the voice mail again. Confused, she left a quick message for Audrey to call her back.

After loading her belongings into her car, she decided to call Mrs. Jennings, Audrey's mother.

Natalie waited for the first ring before lowering herself into her car and starting it up. The air conditioner was already on its highest setting, but even with the cold air pumping out of the vents, it took a while to cool her car.

Mrs. Jennings answered on the third ring. "Hi, Natalie. How are you doing?"

"Hi, Mrs. Jennings. I'm calling to see if you came by and picked up Audrey after she was done surfing?"

"No, Audrey drove her own car to the beach this morning. Isn't she with you?"

"Actually, she left the beach about half an hour before me to get ready for her date with Keith. I'm at the church parking lot where her car is, but she isn't here. The church doesn't appear to be open, and our cars are the only ones here. I thought maybe her vehicle didn't start and you or Mr. Jennings came to pick her up."

There was a pause on the other end of the phone. "Well, no. Mr. Jennings is out on Lake Ashby fishing with some friends from work, and I haven't heard from Audrey since she left the house to meet up with you. Are you sure she isn't there? Did you check to see if she went inside the church? Maybe she needed to use the restroom before coming home."

"Okay, let me go check." Natalie locked her car before walking over to the church's main entrance. Mrs. Jennings continued to wait on the other end of the line.

When Natalie got to the tinted glass doors that faced out to the parking lot, she pulled hard on both handles. But they wouldn't budge. She leaned in and pressed her forehead against the glass to get a better look, but there wasn't a soul in sight.

Having visited this church during a friend's graduation party, she knew of a second entrance on the south side of the building.

But when she got to it, she found that door was locked as well. "Mrs. Jennings, the church doors are locked. I don't think Audrey is here. Could she have called Keith for a ride home?"

"I suppose that's possible. Let me try Audrey's cell phone first. If I can't reach her, then I'll give Keith a call and get back to you." She hung up.

Natalie stood in the same spot for a moment, wondering what happened to her friend in such a short period of time.

Retracing her steps back to her car, she spotted something in her peripheral view—a familiar object in the shrubs nearby.

The shrubbery was up against the building. At over six feet high, the hedges towered over Natalie. Nevertheless, they had been trimmed so their bottom branches appeared to be hovering six inches off the ground.

Natalie had passed these shrubs just minutes ago, but now she was taking more notice of her surroundings for clues to her friend's whereabouts. She ambled over to the shrubs and got on her hands and knees to get a closer look—only to have her suspicions confirmed.

Not only was Audrey's surfboard behind the shrubs, but Natalie reached past the branches and yanked out the beach bag Audrey had with her when she left the beach. Inside were Audrey's towel, cell phone, car keys, and wallet. Natalie stared at the items knowing there wasn't a good reason for them to be hidden.

As Natalie got to her feet, her phone rang, making her jump.

"Natalie, I'm starting to get worried. I tried Audrey's cell phone three different times, but it goes straight to voice mail. Keith said he hasn't spoken with Audrey since this morning. Something isn't right." There was an unmistakable quiver in her voice.

"Mrs. Jennings, I found Audrey's surfboard and beach bag here in the shrubs next to the church. All her belongings, including her cell phone, are in it. And her cell phone has been turned off. I agree things don't look right. I hate to say it, but I think you should call Mr. Jennings and maybe even the police."

Mrs. Jennings gasped. With a trembling voice, she replied, "Okay, I will."

"I'm driving over to your house to help in any way I can."

When they hung up, Natalie rushed to her car and dropped Audrey's beach bag in her passenger seat next to her own belongings. Forgetting all about the surfboard, she sped off to Audrey's house.

It only took a moment for her vision to blur with unshed tears.

# Chapter 3

After crying for what felt like hours, Audrey decided she needed to do something productive—like finding another way to escape besides the air vent. *Maybe something in this room can be used to break open the door.*

But she needed light to see her options. Whoever locked her in here knew what they were doing. *How many other girls have been left in this darkness? Am I the first or has he kidnapped others? And if there were others, what happened to them?*

That was a dark hole of possibilities that didn't do her any good to think about.

Audrey was ripped from her thoughts when she heard the locks on the other side of the door being undone. Her heart started pounding. Before she could stop the thoughts, she was envisioning the very worst. *What do they want from me? Are they going to rape or kill me—or both?!* The bile in her stomach started making its way up her throat. She swallowed hard to stop its trek.

There must've been at least five different locks on the door, because it felt like an eternity for it to finally swing open. Audrey sat against the wall and held her breath as a sliver of light filtered into the room. The light confirmed what her prior search had revealed: there wasn't anything in this small concrete space except the mattress she was on, the bucket (aka toilet), a roll of toilet paper, and a bottled water.

The tall figure emerging through the doorway was wearing a black ski mask, black scrubs, black gloves, and heavy work boots.

Audrey was horrified at the sight of her kidnapper. The masked man was holding a plate in one hand, but his body was blocking the light, making it still too dim for her to see what was on the plate.

As he approached, Audrey quickly sized him up. She guessed he was six feet two and over two hundred pounds. He wasn't much taller than her, but he appeared to be broad with muscular arms. Her eyes widened as he got closer. There was nothing she could do to protect herself so she sat in fear waiting for him to say something, or worse, make physical contact.

"You're awake," said the stranger. His voice held no sympathy for Audrey's situation.

While she didn't recognize his voice, it was possible he was using a fake one to throw her off. She continued to stare at him, trying to hide her terror. Unknowingly, she was holding her breath. She let it out slowly then took another deep gulp of air, while her eyes followed his every move.

Halfway in the room, he stopped.

At this point, Audrey forced herself to take her eyes off his mask and creepy eyes and looked down at his hands. Now that there was enough light in the room, she could see he was carrying a plate of food.

He placed it on the floor in the middle of the room, a couple of yards away from the mattress.

Audrey's mind was racing, and her heart was beating uncontrollably. *What's he going to do next?*

He glared back at her for a moment before slowly backing away from the food. "You better eat. Drink the water too." He motioned to the bottle near the bucket.

Audrey glanced down at the plate of chicken nuggets, plain potato chips, and container of applesauce and looked back up at him. She couldn't find her voice.

"You better eat it," he repeated with narrowed eyes.

She looked again at the food and wondered why he wanted her to eat. *Why does he care if I eat or go hungry? Did he poison it? Is it laced with something that'll knock me out again?*

The sudden realization that he might've done awful things to her when she was out cold made her sicker than she already had been. *Did he take advantage of me while I was unconscious? Would he ever admit to it if he did?*

She'd have to be careful with any food or drink he left for her.

Sensing that he wasn't going to say anything else to her, Audrey found the courage to timidly ask, "Who are you and why am I here?" Again, she held her breath waiting for his response.

While the stranger must've heard her, instead of answering, he gave her a frightening smirk that could scarcely be seen through the mouth hole in the mask.

Even though she didn't want to spend any more time with this stranger than she must, she continued. "If you're hoping to ask for money in exchange for me, I have to tell you my parents aren't rich. But, if you drop me off somewhere, I can find my way home, and no one has to know you took me."

Her kidnapper continued to stare at her.

Audrey became more uncomfortable by the second.

Then he finally answered, "It's none of your business who I am, and you're here because I want you here. When that changes, then you no longer will be."

Audrey didn't know how to respond, and even if she did, she probably wouldn't have had the nerve to say it.

Obviously finished with the conversation, the stranger turned around and headed for the door.

Uncertain that he'd ever return, and out of sheer panic, Audrey jumped up from the mattress and lunged for the door.

As if he knew her thoughts before she did, the masked man swung around. In what felt like one swift move, he caught hold of her upper arms and threw her backwards onto the mattress as though she weighed nothing.

"Don't even think about it! You better behave, or I'll make the next nine months hell for you! You'll be begging me to kill you."

Cowering in the corner, Audrey instantly believed him.

He turned around as if what he said would keep her on the mattress. He left the room and locked the door behind him.

With nothing but the darkness around her, Audrey was thankful he didn't do more than throw her onto the mattress. She knew it was stupid to try getting away without a plan, but she hadn't been thinking clearly.

When her anxiety subsided and her breathing became less labored, she found herself fixating on something he said. *Why did he mention nine months?* Was it possible he knew the secret she hadn't told anyone, not even her parents, boyfriend, or best friend? *How can that be?* Yet, why else did he intend on holding her here for nine months and insist she eat?

There could only be one answer. But then he couldn't have known she was pregnant when he kidnapped her. Did he have other plans for her but had since changed them? And if so, what did he intend to do with her child once he or she was born?

Whatever it was, it wouldn't end well for Audrey. She would never give her child up to this stranger without a fight.

There was no stopping the tears that flowed when she realized she might have to endure months in this room, to eventually die while trying to save the future of her child.

# Chapter 4

Mrs. Jennings wiped away her tears before she quickly dialed her husband's cell phone number. Then she paced her kitchen while anxiously waiting for the first ring.

"Hi, sweetie. We're finishing up on the boat and waiting for our turn to pull up to the dock. It was a busy day out on the water. Looks like everyone had the same idea of being out on their boats today. I'll be home in about an hour, depending on traffic. I didn't catch anything worth bringing home, but there's always next time," came Mr. Jennings's carefree voice.

The fact that he was rambling on about his day didn't surprise his wife. He had always been known for his gift of gab. Mrs. Jennings didn't know how to tell him about their daughter so she allowed him to finish.

"Daniel, something has happened. Audrey hasn't come home. Natalie called and said Audrey's car is still at the church parking lot by the beach, but Natalie can't find her anywhere. I called Keith, but he hasn't heard from her either."

Mrs. Jennings took a deep breath before she continued. "And there's more. Audrey's beach bag full of her belongings was found in some bushes by the church. Her surfboard was there too."

It took a minute for Mr. Jennings to register what his wife was telling him. "Okay, where are Keith and Natalie now?"

"Natalie will be here anytime; she said she was heading over to help. Keith's at home waiting for a call back from me."

"Okay, when Natalie gets there the two of you head to the police station, and I'll meet you there as soon as I can. Call Keith back and tell him to also meet us there. Honey, everything's going to be okay. Audrey will probably show up before the police even take our information."

The couple exchanged "I love yous" before ending the call.

After explaining the situation to his work buddies, Mr. Jennings impatiently waited for their turn to dock.

Fifteen minutes later the boat was tied off. He quickly disembarked and rushed to his silver Chevy Silverado truck. He sped off toward the police station which was thirty minutes away.

Alone in his truck, he began to weep.

# Chapter 5

A few minutes to seven at night, Detective Darryl Harris strolled into the Cocoa Beach precinct and went straight to the kitchen to pour his fourth cup of coffee for the day. With phone messages and emails to catch up on, caffeine was essential for him to get back into his routine.

Being forced to take last week off for his own "mental well-being"—his boss's exact words—Darryl was ready to jump back into his work. He had always taken pride in what he did, even before he was promoted to detective nearly a decade ago at the ripe age of twenty-four.

His desk was one of ten other desks in the main room of the police station, right off the entrance to the precinct. But since his promotion to detective, he didn't spend much time at the station. Darryl only stopped by the precinct to check his emails or voice messages, process paperwork, interrogate suspects, or meet with Captain Reynolds to discuss details of his recent cases. Otherwise, he was at crime scenes questioning witnesses or in other spots around the county following up on leads.

The focus of his attention for the last five years has been seven related cases, which had gone cold a year and a half ago. But Darryl couldn't stop thinking about the killer that was still out there.

With no new evidence or leads in over a year, Darryl was completely consumed with going over the same details day after day. His whole world revolved around the serial killer who had done unspeakable things to the young women he kidnapped, then murdered months later. There wasn't a weekend, holiday, vacation, or birthday that Darryl didn't eat, sleep, and breathe those cases. Even before the cases went cold, his marriage of over ten years had ended because of his obsession with catching the Cocoa Beach Killer.

Then came the recent request for him to take time off. It was more of an order than a request, since his Captain told him to leave the precinct and not come back for at least a week.

As if he had been watching Darryl through the blinds in his office, Captain Reynolds yelled, "Harris, come see me in my office."

*Looks like my phone messages will have to wait.* Darryl picked up his coffee mug and passed by the other desks as he made his way to his boss's office on the other side of the police station.

The door was wide open as Captain Brian Reynolds was reviewing some paperwork on his desk. Not wanting to disrupt his boss's focus, Darryl took a seat and waited.

"How was your week off? You know you can take more time if you need," Captain Reynolds said as he looked up. His piercing blue eyes roamed Darryl's face.

Darryl wasn't sure what he was searching for. Possibly a sign that he was rested or less tense. Since Darryl didn't see the need for the time off to begin with, he replied, "It was fine. And no, I don't need any more time off. Thanks for the offer though. What have I missed?" He sat forward in his chair, eager for the topic of conversation to change. Sitting through another lecture on how he needed to put aside his work and have a personal life was not how he wanted to start his first day back.

Letting out a slow breath, Captain Reynolds said, "There's been a recent development. We're still taking down the details from the parents and the best friend who saw her last, but an eighteen-year-old by the name of Audrey Jennings hasn't been seen since around one this afternoon. Her car is parked at the Methodist church parking lot over on Neptune Avenue, but she's nowhere to be found." He ran his hands through his gray feathered hair.

With furrowed brow, Darryl replied, "It's only been," he paused to glance at his watch, "six hours since she's last been seen. Why are we spending any time looking for an adult? She could've gone off with another friend or called a cab for a ride."

The department's protocol was to wait twenty-four hours before assuming foul play when someone this age appeared to be missing. Technically, Audrey was considered an adult at the age of eighteen. *She doesn't have to check in with her parents every time she changes her plans.*

"Her belongings were found abandoned behind some shrubs at the church. Her best friend brought in the bag with the personal items so I had them sent over to the medical examiner's office to be processed. I also sent officers to the church parking lot to take pictures and search the area for any clues to her whereabouts."

Captain Reynolds watched as Darryl's face changed from wrinkled brow to wide-eyed. He was now making the connection between his cold cases and Audrey's disappearance.

"Like I said, we're still getting information from the parents and from the best friend who saw her last, but from what we've gathered so far, it doesn't look good for Ms. Jennings. I thought you might want to take part in the interviews, if you feel ready to jump in so soon after being away."

"Yeah, that sounds good. Thanks." Darryl couldn't help thinking, *Could the same guy be back at it after all this time?* If so, maybe they have a jump start on the case—something they didn't have with the previous cases. *Maybe after a hiatus from torturing and murdering victims, the killer will mess up this time. Maybe he'll leave valuable evidence behind . . .*

*Lots of maybes, but they could add up to a possible lead.*

# Chapter 6

Audrey rolled over on the mattress for the hundredth time. She hadn't been able to rest since waking up in this gloomy place. It had been a few hours since the kidnapper brought her food. Worst of all, he left her with more questions than answers with his short responses.

Her stomach started to growl. While she was able to resist the chicken nuggets and plain potato chips lying untouched on the paper plate on the floor, Audrey gave in to the plastic container of applesauce. Its foil cover protected it from tampering. At least it didn't look like it had been opened, and Audrey knew she needed to eat something. If not for her, for the baby's sake. She also inspected the cap to the bottled water. Feeling confident it hadn't been tampered with either, she drank the whole bottle.

With no other means to relieve herself, Audrey was forced to use the bucket. She hoped she wouldn't have to do anything more than pee in it. Her body, including her scalp, itched from the dried ocean salt water she hadn't been able to shower off since leaving the beach. Still, these were the least of her worries.

The absence of utensils with her food made Audrey wonder if the masked man didn't leave behind anything that could be used as a weapon against him. Possibly because this wasn't his first kidnapping.

*Maybe he really did bring other girls here before me.* She grew queasy at the thought.

How was she going to cope with living in this darkness with barely any trustworthy food or water, no shower, and without anything to do but sleep? If her kidnapper planned on keeping her alive for the next nine months, then there was time to think of a way out of this. Sadly, though, nine months was not the reality.

Audrey had discovered she was pregnant three weeks ago. When she went over the timing in her head, it became apparent her Fourth of July with Keith had resulted in the pregnancy.

She had planned on telling Keith tonight at dinner. She hadn't told a soul about the baby, not even Natalie. It had been difficult to keep the secret from her best friend. But there was so much to think about. She and Keith were going off to college in different states. On top of that, he was only nineteen years old, and Audrey would only be nineteen at her next birthday, in October. *If I live that long.*

*Will Keith and my family find out about the baby at the same time they're notified of my death?* Her heart physically hurt at the possibility. She couldn't let that happen. No matter what, she was going to get out of this place and deliver a healthy baby. She and Keith would figure out the rest from there. She was certain they loved each other and would make a happy home for their child.

Just as she was attempting to get some sleep, a lock on the other side of the door started to turn.

Audrey sat up on the mattress and waited for the light. This time she planned to examine her surroundings for a way out. *Can I do it without being obvious?* Her one and only encounter with the kidnapper didn't give her any hints to his intentions. She'll need to stay on guard with him.

As the door opened, Audrey surveyed the ceiling and saw the air vent above her head. It was far too high to get to with the few resources in this room. And besides the lonely light bulb in the middle of the ceiling, it was the only other thing she could see above her.

"Didn't eat much did you? Guess the food isn't good enough for you," he sneered. "Maybe this meal will be more to your liking."

After looking from the plate in the middle of the room to the empty applesauce container and water bottle next to the mattress, he added, "At least you drank the water. Guess I didn't waste my time bringing more." He set down two water bottles and exchanged the old plate of chicken nuggets and potato chips with another plate containing a sandwich of some sort, carrot sticks, and a banana.

33

Audrey noticed he was keeping an eye on her during the whole process. Her actions earlier, with trying to flee the room, have him on high alert. *It'll be harder to escape with him watching my every move.* The thought of having to wait to make her escape made her light-headed.

Before he retreated from the room, Audrey got up the courage to ask, "What do you want from me?" When he didn't reply and turned to walk out of the room, she persisted. "You couldn't have known about the baby before you kidnapped me. What are you planning to do when the baby is born?"

He spun around to face her. "So, you've figured out I know your dark little secret. Well, what I plan to do with you or that bastard of yours is *my* secret. All you have to do is behave and eat whatever I bring you."

Audrey's heart was beating faster. "How did you find out? I never told anyone."

He stared at her for a long moment as if deciding whether he should reveal this information. Then with a smirk from behind the mask he said smugly, "You mumbled 'Please don't hurt my baby' when you were partially unconscious. At first, I didn't think I heard you right, but you repeated it two more times."

Content with the baffled look on her face at this response, he walked out the door and locked it behind him.

Audrey sat there staring at the door. *Is he lying? Did I really say that when I was unconscious?* Then she reasoned he couldn't have found out any other way.

Now that she had confirmed he knew about the pregnancy, she had to get him to disclose his intentions for her and her child. *Will he ever slip up and say what he wants with me and the baby?*

It was only possible if she could keep conversation with him going longer than she had in their first two encounters. That was the only thing she was certain of at this point.

# Chapter 7

Captain Reynolds led Darryl through the main room of the police station toward the interview room next to the more closed-off interrogation rooms. After opening the door, he extended his arm to motion for Darryl to enter the room ahead of him.

Sitting with their chairs facing the door, Mr. and Mrs. Jennings both looked up. Mr. Jennings had a somber expression, and his left arm was draped around his wife's shoulders.

Mrs. Jennings had been crying. Her eyes were bloodshot, and she held a rumpled tissue in her right hand.

*Always a hard scene to observe, even for the most veteran of officers*, Darryl noted to himself.

"Mr. and Mrs. Jennings, this is Detective Darryl Harris. He'll be working with officers in the search for your daughter."

At Captain Reynolds's introduction, Darryl shook their hands. He could feel Mrs. Jennings's hand trembling in his.

After Darryl took a seat across the table from the couple, Captain Reynolds quietly left the room, shutting the door behind him.

Picking up the legal pad and pen sitting on the table, Darryl said, "Mr. and Mrs. Jennings, I'm going to do my best to help get Audrey back home safe and sound. To assist in the investigation, I have some questions to ask if that's okay?"

The couple slowly nodded.

"When was the last time you saw Audrey?"

"This morning, before she headed to the beach to meet up with Natalie, her best friend. They were going surfing," Mrs. Jennings answered.

"I left early this morning to go fishing with some buddies from work. That was around seven. Audrey was already awake and making herself some toast for breakfast," Mr. Jennings added.

Jotting the details down, Darryl continued. "Audrey's best friend, Natalie Anderson, she was the last to see Audrey, is that correct?" Captain Reynolds had shared this information with him already, but Darryl wanted to see if any new details came up.

"Yes, Natalie was the one who called me from the parking lot where Audrey's car was parked," Mrs. Jennings replied with a crack in her voice.

Her husband gave her arm a comforting squeeze.

"Natalie came with me to the station, but the officers told her to wait out there," she said, pointing in the direction of the lobby.

It was protocol to interview family and friends separately when investigating a possible kidnapping. Darryl planned on questioning the best friend next. And even though he had a couple more questions for the parents, he didn't plan on keeping them much longer. There was a possibility a ransom call would come, and they all needed to prepare for that.

"Have you noticed anything different about Audrey's behavior or actions lately? Did she seem distant or unsocial?" Darryl worded his questions carefully. His gut was telling him this wasn't a runaway case. But he couldn't jump to the conclusion his serial killer was back either. There were still too many unknowns.

"I wouldn't say she's been distant as much as she's been busy with work and getting ready for college. Audrey was accepted to the University of Florida. She was awarded a volleyball scholarship," Mrs. Jennings explained with a smile filled with pride.

Darryl noticed that Mr. Jennings appeared unsure—as if there was something he suddenly remembered. "Is there anything you want to add, Mr. Jennings? Anything that you think may be important?"

Adjusting in his chair, Mr. Jennings said, "For the last week Audrey hasn't looked well. I heard her getting sick one morning as I passed the guest bathroom. She said it was just a stomach bug, so I told her if her symptoms persisted we would get her to the doctor. It probably isn't worth bringing up, but Audrey has always been a healthy kid. Seemed out of sorts for her." A flash of embarrassment crossed his features when his wife glanced over at him with questioning eyes.

Darryl wondered why he had kept this information from his wife. "Is Audrey your only child or does she have siblings?"

"Audrey is our only child. You have to find her. Please," Mrs. Jennings pleaded.

"She wouldn't have run away. We know she was taken against her will," Mr. Jennings said.

As he wrote down the last of his notes, Darryl asked, "Does Audrey have any social media accounts that you know of?"

Mrs. Jennings replied, "No, she's never been interested in those. Why?"

"There could've been posts or pictures that could've helped in the investigation, that's all." With no more questions to ask the Jennings at this point, Darryl decided it was time to interview Natalie Anderson.

"Mr. and Mrs. Jennings, if the officers have taken down all your contact information, then you can return home. If you think of anything else that may be of help, please give me a call." Darryl handed them a business card that he had fished out of his back pocket. "I believe a team is being sent to your home to put a tap on your phone in case a ransom call comes in."

Mrs. Jennings's eyes went wide.

"It's just procedure," Darryl assured her. "Also, it's important one of you stays home to answer the phone, just in case."

Mrs. Jennings held back a sob behind her tissue.

When Mrs. Jennings had confirmed she was ready to leave, she and Mr. Jennings followed the detective through the main area of the precinct. As they came around the corner of the lobby, a young blonde woman and tall, dark-haired young man sitting on the bench nearest the doors stood to embrace the older couple.

"Detective Harris, this is Natalie Anderson." As they shook hands, Mrs. Jennings extended her hand to rest on the young man's arm. "And this is Keith Lennox, Audrey's boyfriend."

It was clear to Darryl the best friend had been crying. She not only had puffy eyes, but she was still sniffling, even after their introductions.

The boyfriend also appeared distraught as he shifted his weight from one foot to the other. *He might not have seen Audrey as recently as Natalie, but he could have information that'll be useful in the investigation.*

"Ms. Anderson, I need to ask you a few questions. But it shouldn't take too long."

Natalie replied, "Of course."

Then he turned to Keith. "When I'm finished talking with Ms. Anderson, I'll bring you back for some questions."

"Sure, whatever will help find Audrey." Keith sat back down on the bench, while Natalie followed the detective to the interview room.

"Please have a seat, Ms. Anderson," Darryl said as he closed the door.

"You can call me Natalie."

He gave her an acknowledging smile.

When they were both seated, Darryl grabbed the legal pad and pen from where he left them. "I gather you and Ms. Jennings are close. Have you known each other a long time?"

"Her name is Audrey, and yes, we've been best friends since kindergarten." Natalie sat up straighter, waiting for the next question.

Darryl found her tone to be both agitated and impatient. "I'm sorry, am I keeping you from something?" He knew from experience he couldn't get the answers he needed if someone's mind was elsewhere.

"My best friend is missing, and we're sitting here chatting while someone could be out there at this very moment hurting her!" The last part of her statement caused her to choke up. Tears pooled in her eyes.

"It wasn't my intention to upset you. As soon as I'm done with my questions for you and Mr. Lennox, I'll be heading to the church parking lot to help officers gather evidence and look for any possible witnesses. I wouldn't ask the questions if they weren't important to finding Audrey." He got up from his seat to get a tissue from the box on a nearby counter and handed one to her.

She accepted it with a shaky hand. "I shouldn't have shouted. I'm sorry. I'm just so scared for Audrey."

"No need to apologize. How about we move on with the questions?"

She nodded as she wiped away tears.

"Was there anything different in Audrey's mood this morning or anything out of the ordinary she may have said or done?"

Natalie considered this while staring at the table. The struggle on her face made him think she was contemplating whether she should tell him something or not.

"No matter how small or insignificant you may think it is, it might be helpful," Darryl encouraged.

She took a deep breath. "It's been a few weeks since Audrey and I hung out. At the beach this morning, I could tell something was on her mind. In between surfing we talked mostly about silly stuff. But occasionally I'd catch Audrey staring off into space with a sad expression. I asked if she was okay, but she basically said she had a lot going on with college and her move to Gainesville."

"Do you have reason to believe Audrey wasn't telling you the truth? Was there anything else that didn't seem right about her this morning?"

"Honestly, I have no idea what was really bothering her. I'm her best friend, and she couldn't tell me. Do you know how that makes me feel? And now she's gone, and we don't know who has her or what they're doing to her." She started to bawl uncontrollably.

Darryl could tell this interview was over. He pulled another tissue from the box and escorted her out of the room to the lobby where Keith was still waiting.

Jumping up from his seat on the bench, Keith asked, "What happened? Is it Audrey? Have you gotten any news?"

"No. Today's events have taken a toll on Natalie. I'm going to have an officer take her home. I'll be right back."

Darryl approached the front desk and spoke with an officer before returning to Natalie. "They'll have an officer out here momentarily. Go ahead and take a seat on the bench until they're ready for you."

Darryl asked Keith, "Shall we?"

After showing Keith to the same seat Natalie had occupied, Darryl slid into the chair across from him. "I appreciate you waiting."

"Of course."

"So, you've been dating Audrey for some time now, is that correct?"

"Yes, for three years. Her birthday in October will also be our third anniversary." Keith started twisting his hands around the arms of the chair.

"Have you noticed any changes in Audrey's behavior lately? Did anything seem out of the ordinary with her?"

"We haven't seen each other in the last few weeks. Audrey's been busy and hasn't been up for going out."

Darryl wondered what this missing person had going on that she didn't have time for her best friend or her boyfriend. "Besides the fact she didn't have time to hang out, did you notice anything else different about Audrey recently?"

Keith chewed his bottom lip as he mulled over his response. "Last night she said she had something to talk to me about. I thought maybe she was going to break up with me. With her going to college in north Florida and me getting a baseball scholarship to attend Louisiana State, I figured she might not want to continue our relationship long distance."

It was becoming obvious that while something wasn't right in Audrey's life, her family and closest friends didn't seem to know what she was keeping secret.

"Thank you for your time. If you can think of anything else, please give me a call." Darryl pulled out another business card and handed it to Keith.

The detective ushered the youth out of the interview room and back to the lobby entrance. "In case I have any other questions for you, please leave your contact information at the front desk. I appreciate your time," Darryl said as he shook Keith's hand.

With the interviews over, Darryl headed out the door to search the scene of Audrey's last known whereabouts.

# Chapter 8

It was after eight p.m. by the time Darryl pulled into the grassy area on the east side of the church that faced the road. The parking lot on the other side of the building had been roped off with police tape already.

Stepping out of his smoke-gray Dodge Charger, he walked toward the officers searching the scene. He saw someone he recognized right away and ducked under the tape that extended from the side of the building all the way around the perimeter of the parking lot.

"Officer Allen, has any evidence been recovered?" Darryl asked as he pulled on a pair of latex gloves.

Officer Mike Allen smiled. "Hi, detective. They've already retrieved the missing girl's surfboard from the shrubs over there—" he pointed to the west side of the church, "—and we've looked through the vehicle, but there wasn't anything suspicious in it."

"Have you or any of the other officers come across anyone in the area who may have seen something out of the ordinary around here today?"

"Nothing so far. Pastor Ken Fair provided the security tape with today's footage. Maybe that'll give us the person responsible for the girl's disappearance. We've been sweeping the area, but outside of the surfboard, we haven't found anything. If someone did kidnap her, then they knew what they were doing." Officer Allen placed his hands on his slim hips. "Do you think it could be the same guy after all this time?"

It was well known amongst those in local law enforcement that the Cocoa Beach Killer had been picking off girls in their mid- to late teens. After months of physical and sexual abuse, they were murdered and left in semi-secluded areas where they would eventually be found. It was also known that Darryl was the lead detective assigned to the case. And the last known victim was discovered January of last year, leaving no leads to the killer.

"It's always possible, but nothing's conclusive at this point. We still need to determine whether this is a runaway or a kidnapping case. The missing girl is eighteen so she could be choosing not to be found."

Officer Allen nodded. He then nudged Darryl. "Look who was assigned to the case."

Darryl turned to see CSI Mel Crosby arriving to the scene. She had her hair up in a loose bun and just a touch of makeup on. The natural look was extremely attractive on her—or at least it was to Darryl.

As she pulled out her medical bag from the back of the van, she glanced over to see Darryl watching her. Mel gave him a small smile. After locking up the van, she headed in his direction.

"Hi, detective. I figured there was a good chance you were assigned to this case," Mel said, planting herself just inches from him.

"Good evening. Yes, Captain Reynolds has me looking into whether this is a kidnapping case or a runaway situation." He watched her fidget with the bag she was holding and figured she was anxious to process the scene. "Well, I won't hold you up. It's good to see you." Suddenly remembering why they both were there, he added, "Even under these circumstances."

Mel flashed him another smile. "Take care," she said over her shoulder as she made her way to Audrey's car.

Darryl and Mel had seen each other multiple times since their one night together, but she always kept their encounters professional. He thought it was intriguing that she acted as if that night never happened. Intriguing and maybe a bit . . . *disappointing*?

They had gone out late one night after the verdict was announced regarding a double homicide case they had worked on together. The victims were children of a couple of drug addicts who had gotten high and mistook their twin five-year-old boys for intruders. The father shot them dead in the doorway of the master bedroom. It had been an incredibly heartbreaking case to work.

After the case went to trial, the parents were convicted of manslaughter. A group involved in the case went out for drinks. Not to celebrate the win, because there was no win when children had been murdered. It was more of a way of closing the case.

Darryl and Mel's night hadn't ended with drinks at the local bar though. Realizing they had drunk past their legal limit and everyone else had gone home, Mel invited Darryl to share a cab to her apartment—a ten-minute ride away.

The rest was history. At least it seemed so for Mel, but Darryl couldn't get her off his mind.

Getting back to the work at hand, Darryl thanked Officer Allen for the information and began his search. He decided to leave Audrey's car for now, since Mel was processing it for fingerprints, DNA, and other possible evidence. Being around her was starting to be too much of a distraction, and this case might be tied to something bigger.

Darryl walked up to the church doors to see if there were any signs that a struggle took place outside the building. Now that it was getting dark, he pulled his flashlight from his belt and moved the light all around the entryway and down the walkway to the parking lot.

Shining his light into the small bushes that lined both sides of the walkway, he didn't see anything out of sorts. Darryl proceeded to the south side entrance and aimed his flashlight all along the ground near the door. There was nothing out of sorts there either.

As his dark brown eyes roamed the area, he captured a mental blueprint of the property. The south side of the church had a row of large shrubs that separated the property from the shopping plaza directly beyond them. To the north of the church was a side street that led to the parking lot. Past that street was a line of privacy fences blocking view to the nearby houses. To the west, adjacent to the parking lot, was a large vacant lot. And across the street to the east, beyond a two-lane road, was the ramp that led to the beach.

*There are lots of ways in and out of this area for someone who wants to disappear, or for someone who wants to make someone disappear.*

While the security footage from the church could provide answers to Audrey's disappearance, Darryl planned to request the security tape from the stores in the shopping plaza.

Now that it was getting close to nine o'clock, even with his flashlight and the church parking lot lights, it was too dark to do a thorough search. Darryl realized he'd have to wait until tomorrow morning to continue. He didn't like having no leads at this point, especially since so much can happen to a victim in this amount of time. Assuming Audrey had been kidnapped, which they hadn't proved yet.

As he strode back to the front of the church, Darryl spotted a few officers wrapping up and heading out. Mel, however, was diligently processing Audrey's vehicle.

Officer Allen was still standing post nearby.

Ducking under the police tape, Darryl asked, "Are you going to be here for a while?"

The officer noticed Darryl staring in Mel's direction. "Yep, I just got on duty at seven o'clock so I'll be here all night."

"Sounds good. If you get called away for any reason, give me a ring. I may catch some shuteye at the precinct. Call the front desk and have someone wake me up if you can't reach me right away."

When Officer Allen agreed, Darryl felt comfortable taking off. Now that the initial interviews were done, and Audrey's car and personal items were being processed, it was time for him to dive into the personal life of this missing girl.

Based on what her parents, best friend, and boyfriend had told him earlier that day, Audrey was hiding something. If it had to do with her disappearance, Darryl aimed to uncover her secret.

For now, he would go back to the precinct to see what he could find on her electronic devices. Audrey's parents had provided her laptop to officers after his interview with them. The same officers also retrieved items from the home that contained Audrey's DNA.

Darryl wanted to believe that this girl had vanished of her own accord, and that she hadn't fallen victim to the sick bastard he had been hunting for the last five years.

# Chapter 9

Audrey was convinced her first night in this room had come and gone. After dosing on and off for hours, she finally gave up on sleep.

With her hunger growing by the minute, Audrey decided to eat the banana left on the plate from yesterday. The newest water bottles appeared safe so she drank one in between bites of the banana. Feeling less nauseous, she examined the sandwich—peanut butter on whole wheat bread. Having rationalized that she'd need strength to get away from her kidnapper, Audrey took a cautious bite. She waited a few minutes to make sure its contents hadn't been spiked. Not feeling any ill effects, she finished eating it.

Thankful the nausea had subsided, at least for now, she crept back to the mattress to lie down. Since the constant darkness could make a person go crazy, she had learned to close her eyes and think of something other than the depressing room. Memories of the beginning of her relationship with Keith came to mind.

\*\*\*

It had been during their sophomore year in high school. Audrey had always been athletic, excelling in volleyball from the time she was ten. However, Phys Ed hadn't been her favorite class. That changed the semester she met Keith. She thought he was both personable and athletic; a winning combination that made him the kind of boy she could see herself with.

It didn't take long for Audrey to get Keith's attention in return. Flag football had been the game of the week. Audrey was as skilled at running as she was at serving a volleyball. When the teams for flag football were chosen, Keith was picked for one team and Audrey for the other.

After multiple bad throws, some missed catches, and quarterback "sacks" by both teams, the score was 0-0 with only two minutes left in the period. The teams huddled up separately to go over their final plays. As the two sides had made their way back to the line of scrimmage, Keith made sure to pick the spot across from Audrey.

More than pleased to see him in front of her, she looked directly at him and gave him a smile that said, *I dare you.*

"Hike" was called, and seconds later players scattered, doing their best to keep possession of their flags while trying to figure out who would get the football next.

The quarterback on Audrey's team had noticed that the boy player he planned on throwing to was completely covered. He was running out of time to get rid of the ball. Then he saw that Audrey was not only open but was only a few yards from the end zone.

He threw the ball in a decent spiral right to her. When the football made its way into Audrey's arms, Keith was only a yard or so behind her. He watched in amazement as she caught the ball, brought it in to her body, and turned and sprinted for the end zone.

It hadn't taken long for Keith to regain his composure and run after her, swiftly tackling her in the end zone.

Later, classmates asked him if he understood they were playing *flag* football when he jumped Audrey in the end zone.

Keith simply replied, with a sly grin on his face, "Of course."

\*\*\*

The locks on the door start turning, bringing Audrey back to reality. She automatically sat up on the mattress and nervously waited for the door to open.

The masked man entered the room wearing his usual attire, but this time he was holding a long piece of rope and a blindfold.

She stared at the items in horror.

Like any other sadist, he smiled at the fear he evoked. Walking toward her, he kicked the plate of food out of his path with his heavy boot.

"Get up."

Audrey did as he said.

"Hold your arms out straight."

She obeyed.

He wrapped the rope around her wrists and tied the knot tight. Then he slipped the blindfold over her eyes.

Audrey did her best not to panic, but her heart was hammering in her chest. *Is this it? Is he going to take me somewhere to kill me?!*

"We're getting out of here for a few minutes." He clutched the top of her right arm with his gloved hand and led her out of the room.

They must have gone down a narrow hallway, because Audrey's left arm repeatedly hit the wall. His grip on her other arm was so tight it restricted the blood flow.

After her kidnapper pushed open a door, they exited to the outside. Audrey felt the sun beating down on her. She had never been more thankful for a sunny day than she was right now. Tears sprang to her eyes, but she was not going to give her kidnapper the satisfaction of letting them fall.

Since she didn't have a chance to put her flip flops on back in the room, Audrey felt the grass under her bare feet.

Only a few yards farther, he stopped and yanked off her blindfold.

Directly in front of her stood a concrete shower; it reminded her of the showers at the summer camp she attended as a kid. It had three concrete walls, but to her alarm, there was no door or even a curtain. Her stomach started churning at the thought of having to be naked in front of this man.

"There's a towel in there, and a dress to change into after you shower. Supplies are already in there. Don't try to pull any stunts. I'll be watching you," he warned as if the situation wasn't horrible enough.

He untied the rope from her wrists and pushed her toward the concrete structure.

"You want me to shower with you watching?"

*Is he going to try to assault me while I'm naked in there? What can I do to protect myself if he tries to touch me—or worse?!*

"Quit stalling and get in there. You can't stay in those clothes so leave them in the shower when you're done." He gestured for her to move forward.

When she stood rooted in one spot, he added, "Get in the shower or I'll undress you myself, and I won't be gentle about it."

The menace in his eyes told her this wasn't an idle threat.

*There's no way out of it. I have to shower in front of him.*

She managed to get her unwilling limbs to step into the shower and turn on the water. While it warmed up, she slowly peeled off her clothing. In her best attempt at modesty, she kept her back to the stranger. The only view she would give him was of her backside.

Once her shorts, tank top, and bathing suit were off, she kicked them into a corner in front of her. Reaching over to her left, Audrey picked up the toothbrush and toothpaste lying on the high ledge. She had never been so desperate to brush her teeth.

Now that the water was warm enough, she stepped sideways into the stream. When her hair was dampened, she reached over for the shampoo. In doing so, she took a quick glance back to see what the masked man was doing, and even more important, where he was.

While he was still positioned a few yards away from the shower, he stared at her naked body with such intensity shivers ran up her spine.

To get this ordeal over with as soon as possible, Audrey lathered up her hair while holding the toothbrush with her mouth. She rinsed her mouth out with shower water as she rinsed the suds out of her hair.

Stretching her arm to the ledge, she grabbed the white bar of soap sitting next to the shampoo bottle. With minimal movements, she stepped out of the stream of water, lathered up, and precious moments later, she was back under the water.

Even though it took only a few minutes, the shower felt endless. After turning the water off and keeping her back to the masked man behind her, Audrey snatched the towel from the ledge. She couldn't get it around her body fast enough.

She quickly pulled the dress over her head. As she removed the towel, she noticed there were no undergarments on the ledge. Panic started to rise again. *Why is there a dress but no underwear or bra? What's he planning to do to me now that I've showered?!*

As if concerned she might be planning an escape, the stranger stomped over to the shower and pulled her out.

"Where are the rest of the clothes?" she timidly asked as he tied her wrists with the rope.

"You don't need any more clothes."

His response didn't give her any comfort.

With the blindfold over her eyes, he led her back to the room.

Audrey wasn't sure what he planned to do with her clothes, but she couldn't concern herself with them. Her fate once they reached the room was all she could think about.

They headed back through the narrow hallway. After pushing her onto the mattress, he took her mask off and began removing the rope from her wrists.

There seemed to be a battle waging in his head. When he finished removing Audrey's ropes, he glared at her as she sat in front of him. Concern must've shown on her face because he flashed her a sinister smirk, then turned to leave the room. Before he got to the door, he pulled out a simple black comb from his back pocket and threw it on the mattress. Without a word, he shut the door behind him.

Audrey could hear the locks turn and a minute later, silence.

*What was the point of the shower? Why did he allow me to brush my teeth and give me a clean dress to wear? Could this be a game he plays with his victims before he does horrible things to them?*

# Chapter 10

Darryl arrived back at the Methodist church parking lot at approximately eight o'clock the next morning. He had caught a few hours of sleep in the precinct's bunk room. It wasn't the most private of setups. But a detective could have his or her choice of eight different beds with fresh sheets whenever they worked long hours and found a moment to catch some shuteye.

Darryl expected to have Audrey's laptop by now, but it was sent to a Certified Digital Forensics Examiner to get past its password protection. The closest examiner was in Orlando, so he wouldn't get the laptop back for at least a few days, or possibly even a week. He'd have to move forward with finding other leads until her laptop came back.

Once her cell phone was processed, he could send that off as well. Assuming it was also password protected.

It was already hot out at eighty-five degrees and eighty percent humidity. Darryl was more than ready for fall to come, even though cooler weather wouldn't follow for months to come.

Darryl showed his badge to the officer guarding the scene from his patrol car. He then notified the cop he'd be scouring the property.

Slipping on his latex gloves, Darryl began by searching the area around the shrubs where Audrey's personal belongings were found. He was hopeful the medical examiner's office would recover prints from the recovered items, or possibly even some DNA evidence.

When he didn't find anything in or near the shrubs, he crept meticulously along the side of the church, eying the ground for anything out of the ordinary. Coming up empty-handed, Darryl moved on to the bushes that lined the main entrance. He swept aside the branches to search for anything that may have gotten snagged in them or may have fallen through them to the ground below. But nothing was out of place.

Rounding the south corner of the church, he reached the side entrance he had come across the night before. However, there was no evidence of a struggle at this door either.

When he made it around the perimeter of the church, Darryl decided to look through Audrey's car next. While it had been left unlocked, he had to move the police tape that was stretched across the driver's side door.

He slid into the driver's seat, instantly taking in the smell of coconut and raspberries. *Must be Audrey's perfume or body spray.* An initial scan of the missing girl's car told him she was a clean individual. There was no garbage or food of any kind anywhere in the vehicle. In the middle console, Darryl found a cell phone charger and loose change. The glove compartment contained only the car's owner's manual, a small package of Kleenex, and the vehicle's registration.

With no new evidence, Darryl let his mind wander to the reason for his restless slumber last night. Running into Mel had bothered him, and he couldn't figure out why. She wasn't his first one-nighter, or his last. Though he had been divorced for some time now, he still struggled with the idea of getting serious with anyone and risk being hurt again.

His marriage had lasted ten years, but his commitment to the serial killer case ultimately became his priority. Years of coming in second to her husband's career was too much for his ex-wife. She eventually became involved with someone at her office, finally ending their marriage for good.

Even with memories of what he went through in his divorce, he longed to be with Mel.

The CSI was considered tall at five feet eight inches. Her slender physique helped showcase her toned upper arms and thighs. With long brown hair and brown eyes, her olive skin tone gave her an exotic appearance.

It wasn't just her beauty that kept Darryl's interest though. Over the years, he had learned she was not only smart, but she shared many of his same interests—including football. They both were diehard fans of the Tampa Bay Buccaneers, one of Florida's three NFL teams. That was one of the topics of conversation Darryl and Mel had the night they were at the bar, before going back to her place.

In Darryl's mind, Mel was the whole package. If he was ever going to risk heartbreak again, it would be for a chance at a relationship with her. Regrettably, he left her the next morning and never contacted her about that night. A poor choice that may have crushed any opportunity for him to pursue a relationship.

He had no one to blame for that sad realization but himself.

Deciding not to focus any longer on his past faults, Darryl got back to the job at hand. As he climbed out of the car, he caught a glimpse of a surfer walking by the church toward the beach ramp. The young, long-haired blond male had no shoes or shirt on and was carrying a dark-blue surfboard. It was hard to miss his bright yellow-and-blue swim trunks.

*He must've come from somewhere nearby to not have shoes on. If he lives close by, there's a chance going surfing is part of his daily routine.*

"Excuse me, sorry to bother you," Darryl shouted. He caught up to the surfer, who was now waiting at the street corner for the pedestrian light to change.

Darryl lifted his shirt just enough to reveal his badge to the young man. "Can I ask you some quick questions? I promise I won't keep you long."

The surfer looked hesitant, but asked, "Does this have to do with the police tape over there?"

"Yes, there's a missing girl, and I'm investigating her disappearance."

"I don't know if I can be of help but ask away."

"Thank you. Did you happen to come by here yesterday?"

"Yep, I come past here every day to go surfing. I live a few houses that way." The surfer pointed north of the church toward a housing development. "If the weather's decent anyway."

"Did you happen to see anything strange yesterday when you passed by? Or maybe somebody who stuck out to you for any reason?"

The young man's forehead wrinkled in concentration. "Yeah, now that you ask, there was a guy in scrubs standing by the church talking on his phone. He had a ball cap on that was so low I couldn't see his face. He was also wearing boots. I didn't think much of it yesterday, but it's odd, since the church wasn't open at the time. I barely caught sight of him before he walked around the corner of the building and out of view."

"Can you guess as to his height and weight?" Darryl pulled out a small pad he carried in his back pocket. A tiny pencil was intertwined in the wire that kept the pad together.

"He was a lot bigger than me. I'd say he was around six feet two or three and around two hundred twenty or thirty pounds."

Darryl scribbled the details down before asking, "What time was it when you saw this man in scrubs?"

"I was coming back from the beach, so around noon, I think."

*That can't be a coincidence.* He tried not to get too excited at this possible new lead. But Darryl's instincts told him this information confirmed Audrey had been kidnapped. "Did you see where the guy in the ball cap went? Did he have a vehicle nearby?"

"No, I didn't see any other cars, except the two that were there that morning when I was heading to the beach—a white car and a blue one. I see them parked over there often. Probably owned by the two girls who surf out by the beach ramp. I guess the guy in the ball cap must've been dropped off at the church or walked over from somewhere else." The surfer was getting antsy now that the pedestrian light changed yet again.

Darryl wrote down the young man's contact information in case he had more questions for the young man or needed him to identify a possible suspect.

Once the surfer had raced across the street, Darryl called the precinct to provide this information to his boss. *These new details might be enough to move forward with this case as a kidnapping. If so, then there's the possibility the Cocoa Beach Killer is back.*

Captain Reynolds answered the phone.

"Captain, it looks like we have a suspect in the Audrey Jennings's case. I talked to a local surfer, and he saw a guy at the church around noon yesterday who was wearing scrubs and a ball cap. An odd combination. Have we gotten any security film from the stores in the shopping plaza? I want to see if we can get an ID on this guy."

"Managers at all three stores have been contacted, but only one has a security camera that took footage of the outside of the plaza. The gentleman who owns the thrift store is going to have his security tape available today. And I'm glad you called. There's been another development in the case. Why don't you finish up and meet me at the precinct when you're done? I'll fill you in on what has come up."

When he got off the phone, Darryl stood still for a moment as he gazed down the road. He thought it interesting that they've come across two developments in this case at the same time.

*Hopefully at least one of these leads will provide a clue to Audrey's disappearance.*

## Chapter 11

Audrey had been staring at the ceiling for hours—ever since the kidnapper brought her back from the shower. As petrifying an experience as it was, the itching of her skin had subsided, and her nausea had lessened.

Audrey went over the events that had taken place since being kidnapped. The stranger brought her food and bottled waters. Today he allowed her to shower and brush her teeth. The creepy stare he had focused on her while she was showering was scary, but he didn't try to physically assault her. It all added up to keeping her alive and somewhat healthy, at least until she was ready to deliver her baby.

She desperately wanted to know his plans for her child, but at this point, she could use this information to make her situation less dreadful. Then she would make her move to escape.

Shortly after concocting a plan for her next conversation with her kidnapper, the locks on the door began to turn.

To her surprise, he stepped into the room wearing jeans and a black shirt in place of the scrubs he wore on his prior visits. He was still wearing his usual black ski mask, gloves, and boots. In his hand was a plate holding a hot dog in a bun, a small bag of Cheetos, and a medium unpeeled orange. Two bottles of water were tucked under his left arm.

Once the plate and bottled waters were on the floor, he sauntered over to the paper plate he had kicked aside earlier that day. Having picked up the discarded food, he turned to leave, showing no interest in conversing with his victim.

Audrey realized she would need to start the dialogue between them. "If you want this baby to grow healthy, then I need some lights on in here, at least for part of the day. It's depressing sitting in the dark all the time. How do you think that'll affect the baby's growth?"

She waited to see if this was enough of a reason for him to give her light. The request didn't seem like much to her, but the stranger hadn't shown any real concern for her comfort. So Audrey appealed to his interest, which, unnerving as it was, was her unborn child.

Now standing in the doorway with his hand on the doorknob, the stranger narrowed his eyes on her.

*Will he give in or completely ignore my request?*

"I'm not sure if what you're saying is true or not. You could be making that up to get what you want." And without another word, he closed the door and locked it.

*That could've gone worse.*

Since her stomach was growling and there was nothing else to do, Audrey slid off the mattress and located the plate of food on the floor. She chose the bag of Cheetos first, tore it open, and greedily devoured its contents. Picking up one of the bottles of water, she confirmed it hadn't been opened yet. It took her just a few large swigs for the bottle to be half empty. While the nausea came and went, it lessened when she ate.

Even though she didn't enjoy eating hot dogs, Audrey forced herself to take a few bites for the protein. After she snatched the orange, she found her usual spot on the mattress.

*What if he doesn't turn the light on? How long can I take being in here like this? The darkness is maddening.*

She began to cry. *What kind of psycho does this to another human being?* She had nothing to do but eat whatever the masked man brought her, use the five-gallon bucket as a restroom, and sleep the rest of the day. And she couldn't forget the oh-so-creepy shower.

She wondered how often he would take her out of the room to bathe. The only other positive, outside of the hygiene aspect, was that she could get fresh air and sunlight, even if only for a few minutes.

That first shower had been such a demeaning and scary event for her. She hadn't taken the time to observe the area around her for clues to her location or to anyone who could help her escape.

As she made a mental note to do so the next time the stranger took her for a shower, something suddenly happened. The lightbulb on the ceiling turned on! Audrey's eyes slowly adjusted to the brightness. She wondered if the stranger planned on turning the light on every day, even if only for short periods. While there was a chance it wouldn't be on long, she'd take what she could get.

She got up from the mattress and took a better look around the room. She hadn't missed much in the darkness, but in case the light went out soon, she took advantage of the opportunity.

The room was about twenty feet by twenty feet in size with the mattress in the right back corner of the room when looking in from the doorway. The bucket was in the corner nearest the door, adjacent to the mattress. She assumed the bucket was close to the door so her kidnapper didn't have to carry it far to empty it.

Thus far Audrey had used it solely to urinate. The anxiety of being kidnapped and not knowing what the stranger would do at any given moment had resulted in her not needing the bucket outside of that bodily function. There had been times when she thought she might get sick in it. Thankfully, the very little she had eaten recently had stayed down.

*Maybe the nausea will go away soon.* She remembered hearing that most pregnant women only delt with it for the first six to twelve weeks of pregnancy. Now that she was at the seven-week mark, she prayed she wouldn't be sick much longer.

Outside of the plate of food she left sitting in the middle of the room, the space around her was void. The only noise she ever heard in here was from the air whistling through the vent above her.

She stood on her mattress to get a better look at the air vent, but due to the height of the ceiling, she finally ruled it out as an option for escaping. If she couldn't escape while inside the room, then she would need more opportunities outside to get away.

If not for her pregnancy, she'd attempt to get past the masked man when he came into the room next. The sound of the locks being turned gave her plenty of time to get into position behind the door. However, she couldn't put her baby's life in jeopardy. Taking a risk like that could result in her kidnapper killing them both in a fit of rage if her escape wasn't successful.

Audrey was unsure how much his plan for her child outweighed his control over his urges. His plan allowed for her to cover her basic needs. *But will it allow me to get more? How long should I wait to ask for time outside?*

She was granted her last request, but only because it had to do with the well-being of the baby. *Can I get the same outcome when I ask for fresh air and sunlight?* Audrey contemplated this for a few minutes before deciding a day or two wait would give her a better chance at getting her request.

Now she had to find ways to make the time pass until she got that opportunity. Back on the mattress she started to peel the orange. Then it dawned on her: *With the light on I can move around more, and even better, start exercising. This'll allow me to keep up my strength, and possibly give me an upper hand if given the chance to overpower him.*

She smiled at the thought. Her first smile since leaving Natalie at the beach.

# Chapter 12

After spending the morning searching the church parking lot, Darryl drove to the precinct and beelined it to Captain Reynolds's office.

Tapping on his boss's door, Darryl said, "You mentioned something came up in the Jennings's case?"

Reclining backwards in his chair, Captain Reynolds replied, "Yes. Go ahead and take a seat."

"Thanks."

"Ms. Anderson, the missing girl's best friend, stopped by the precinct this morning. Officer Brown took down her information." He handed Darryl a manila folder lying on top of one of the many disheveled piles of paperwork on his desk.

The detective flipped it open and yanked out Officer Brown's notes. After carefully reading them, he cocked an eyebrow. "Natalie thinks her ex-boyfriend is responsible for Audrey's disappearance? Do we know where this Carl Bennett is?"

"When Ms. Anderson was leaving the precinct, I asked her where she thought he'd be on a Saturday afternoon." After a dramatic pause, Captain Reynolds said, "Darryl, he works as a sterilization technician at the hospital. He wears scrubs for work."

He let his words sink in before continuing. "Officer Brown called the hospital and confirmed Carl is working today until three. Officers Allen and Kentz will pick Carl up at the end of his shift and bring him in for questioning. I figure you'll want to do the honors."

Darryl nodded and moved his attention back to the notes. "It says here that Natalie's ex played tight end on their high school football team. He must be a big boy to play that position. He might fit the description of the guy with the ball cap at the church yesterday. And if the information Natalie gave Officer Brown is true, then we have a motive for Audrey's kidnapping."

With a few hours to go before Carl was to be brought in, Darryl decided to go get lunch. It would give him an opportunity to be alone so he could put together an extensive list of questions to ask Carl.

With the case file in hand, he stopped at his desk to check his voice messages. The light on his office phone was flashing. But to his surprise, the only message was from Mel asking him to give her a call at work as soon as he could.

After two rings, she answered, "Brevard County Medical Examiner's Office, Mel speaking."

Her soft voice practically put Darryl in a trance. "Hi, Mel. It's Darryl. You left me a message to call you."

"Yes, thanks for calling me back. I'm finishing my report on the Jennings's case, but I thought you might be interested in hearing what I found now rather than later."

*So, the reason for her call is professional and not personal.* This disappointed him, but he forced his focus back to the call. "Please, go ahead."

"I've processed the missing girl's personal items, and the only prints I found are those of her best friend, Natalie Anderson."

"You're saying Audrey hid her own stuff in those shrubs?"

"No, you don't understand. Natalie's are the *only* prints on the cell phone, car keys, and wallet from the beach bag. And there are *no* fingerprints on the surfboard, not even Audrey's. Someone must've taken the time to wipe them down before hiding them." Mel paused to allow him time to sort out these details.

He quickly caught on. "Okay, so now we have further proof of a kidnapping, but no evidence to help us catch the person. Was there anything found in or around Audrey's vehicle that gives us a lead?"

"I hate to give you more bad news, but no. I'm sorry."

The sincerity in her voice touched him. But then he reminded himself not to read anything into it. "I appreciate your letting me know. I have a suspect to question this afternoon so that may lead to a break in this case yet." He thanked her for the information before they hung up.

Mel didn't have to take the time to call and personally notify him of her findings. He'd receive a copy of her report by the end of the day, or by tomorrow morning at the latest. *Is it possible she still has interest in me after all this time? It seems like a long shot.*

Coming back to his senses, he collected his car keys and headed out to lunch.

Since they hadn't recovered even a trace of physical evidence from the parking lot or Audrey's personal items, Darryl needed to come up with the right questions to get his newest suspect to talk. If Carl was the kidnapper he was looking for, then this could be his only shot at nailing him for the crime. And getting Audrey back before she was seriously hurt.

Three miles down the road, Darryl ordered his chicken salad sandwich and chips from the local food truck. Since the truck was parked most days on a paved lot near the beach ramp, the detective occasionally sat at the covered benches nearby. The location allowed him to get away from the noise of the precinct and think more clearly. With the significance of his next interrogation on his mind, he wanted to be at the top of his game. It could mean the difference between life or death for a young woman.

Two hours had gone by, during which time Darryl had finished his lunch and compiled a list of questions. He felt confident his questions would either trip Carl up if he was guilty of Audrey's kidnapping or would prove his innocence.

If he was honest with himself, Darryl didn't know where to go next with this case if Carl was a dead end. The thought of another girl falling victim to a serial killer who got away from him a year and a half ago both angered and worried him.

*It's time to get this interrogation under way.*

\*\*\*

Officers Allen and Kentz showed up to the precinct around three thirty with Carl Bennett in their possession. The two officers had been mistaken for brothers on multiple occasions, with their similar style crew cuts, lean physiques, and matching heights of five feet ten inches.

Darryl was sitting in front of his computer when they arrived. Watching the officers escort Carl through the main room—Officer Kentz leading the way and Officer Allen bringing up the rear—Darryl noticed the suspect had a scowl on his face. The detective was confident that the big guy was a good fit for the surfer's description of the man at the church.

After depositing the suspect in one of the rooms, Officer Allen strolled over to Darryl's desk. "Carl Bennett is ready for you in interrogation room one. Good luck, he's a hothead. He only came along willingly when we told him he was going to be questioned about Audrey Jennings's disappearance. Just thought you should know."

"Thanks for the heads-up. He's quite a large man. I'll have to keep that in mind in case I make him mad," Darryl joked.

Officer Allen chuckled as he walked away.

Darryl took this as his cue to join Carl in the interrogation room. He gathered his pad and pen before taking off in that direction.

As Darryl opened the door, he was greeted with crossed arms and a hateful glare. Since the suspect was sitting in the chair that faced the door, Darryl glanced under the table to see that Carl was wearing green scrubs and black Nike tennis shoes. The young man was built like a fridge at approximately six feet three inches and over two hundred forty pounds. Darryl mentally compared Carl's red hair and freckles to an oversized Cabbage Patch doll.

Darryl lowered himself into a chair. "Mr. Bennett, my name is Detective Darryl Harris. Did the officers explain why you've been brought in today for questioning?" *Of course they did*. But he wanted to gauge Carl's demeanor with a simple question.

"They said Audrey Jennings is missing and I can help with the investigation by answering some questions. But I don't know what to tell them, or you for that matter, that'll help find her. This is a big waste of my time."

Now that he had tested the suspect's mood, Darryl determined it best to ease into his questioning rather than send this guy off on a tangent that wouldn't get Darryl any answers. "You just finished your shift at the hospital and want to go home and relax, I would imagine. I'll try to get through the questions as fast as I can so the officers can drive you back to the hospital to get your vehicle."

Carl had a less hostile look on his face as he sat up straighter in his seat and set his hands in his lap.

"I see you wear scrubs for work. Do you normally wear those tennis shoes to work as well?"

"Yes, always."

"Yeah, I suppose they're the most comfortable option when you stand on your feet as much as you do," Darryl noted before moving on to his next question. "Do you work full time at the hospital?"

"I started working full time at the beginning of the summer. I work four ten-hour shifts a week."

"Are you one of the lucky folks who has a set schedule or is it like most people's schedules who work in hospitals, and it changes week by week?" Darryl was trying to determine if Carl had an alibi for the previous day. If not, he'd have to move forward with more personal questions that were sure to get the big guy upset.

"It changes week by week, but that's not what you want to know."

Darryl heard the accusation in the suspect's voice and realized Carl was smarter than Darryl gave him credit for. "Okay, then tell me if you worked a shift yesterday during the hours of noon and two p.m. And if so, who can vouch for that?"

Carl's focus dropped to his hands in his lap.

"If you didn't work yesterday, is there *anyone* who can vouch for your whereabouts at the time Audrey went missing?"

Finally looking up, Carl nervously said, "No, I was alone during that time. It was my day off, and I was playing video games all day. My folks are out of town visiting my grandmother in Baltimore. They've been gone since last weekend."

Carl finished this statement with a certain expression on his face. Not guilt—more like fear. *Is it an act or is he truly worried he doesn't have an alibi?*

"It has been brought to my attention that you and your girlfriend broke up recently. Can you tell me why?" This was the start of Darryl's harder questions. He'd need to choose them wisely if he was going to keep a dialogue going with his suspect.

"So, you've been talking with Natalie. Is that why I'm here? She's still mad at the fact I had feelings for Audrey. That explains it then." He let out a cynical laugh.

Attempting to move the topic off Carl's ex and back to Audrey, Darryl asked, "Was Audrey aware of your feelings for her?"

This question ignited a flame in the suspect as fury reflected in his eyes. "Yes, I admitted my feelings to her shortly after my breakup with Natalie. I figured she'd tell Audrey, and I wanted to explain my feelings to her personally."

"What did Audrey say when you told her how you felt?"

An anguished laugh rose before Carl nearly shouted, "That bitch told me I was an asshole for hurting Natalie, and she'd never feel for me what I did for her!"

The change in the young man's mood immediately threw up red flags. If Carl was responsible for Audrey's disappearance, then Darryl needed to "poke the bear" to get him to admit guilt. "That must've made you angry. You must've been extremely hurt by her rejection." He reclined back in his chair and waited for the young man's reaction.

However, the anger in the young man suddenly subsided rather than intensified. Shaking his head, he replied, "It wasn't like that. Yeah, it hurt that she didn't feel the same way about me. But it hurt more when I later realized I lost a great girlfriend for nothing. I didn't even fight to keep my relationship with Natalie. I miss her, but I don't know how to make things right."

This last part came out in a whisper that Darryl almost didn't catch.

The detective felt a bolt of guilt at feeling the same way about his situation with Mel. "You're saying you didn't feel the need to get back at Audrey for how she treated you?"

"Of course not. I know things don't look good for me, not having an alibi and all, but I didn't have anything to do with Audrey going missing. Besides, it's not like I was the only admirer she had outside of her boyfriend. When I went to her volleyball match the night I told her how I felt, I saw a guy practically staring holes into her while she played."

Darryl's head shot up. "There was a man at the game staring at Audrey? What did he look like?"

"He was older. Probably around his late twenties or early thirties. He was clean shaven with dark hair and green eyes. Tall—maybe six feet three—and easily weighed less than two hundred pounds. He reminded me of Audrey but the guy version of her. He was wearing a suit and tie, which is what caught my eye to begin with. Nobody wears clothes that nice to a high school volleyball match. Not even the working parents."

"When was this?"

"It was toward the end of the school year, in mid-May," Carl answered. "It was one of her last matches."

Darryl was puzzled. *If someone was watching Audrey three months ago, why did it take this long for him to kidnap her? He couldn't find an opportunity sooner than that?*

"You said he looked like a male version of Audrey? Is it possible he was a family member? Maybe a cousin or uncle?"

"I guess it's possible, but he left before her game was over. Seems strange he didn't stick around after the game to congratulate her if they were related."

"Where was this game played?" Darryl figured he'd need to get security footage—if there was any.

"Melbourne High School."

The detective got these details down on paper. Since Audrey's parents had already called the police station multiple times since interviewing with him yesterday, Darryl decided he would bring them in for an update and ask them a few more questions. They'll either confirm someone resembling Audrey was at the game, or they'd put a larger spotlight on Carl as a suspect.

"Okay, Carl, I think that's it for now. If you think of more details regarding the guy at the game, please give me a call." He handed Carl a business card before escorting him to the officers waiting to give him a ride back to his car.

As Carl was halfway out the main doors of the precinct, Darryl hollered, "Don't leave the area, in case I have more questions for you."

# Chapter 13

Mrs. Jennings answered the phone. "Hello, this is Margaret."

"Hi, this is Detective Harris. Would you and Mr. Jennings be able to come down to the precinct? I have an update on Audrey's case, and I also want to ask you a few more questions."

"Yes, yes, of course. We'll be right there." She quickly hung up.

A few minutes later, Captain Reynolds was coming back late from lunch.

Darryl jumped out of his chair and trailed after him into his office. "Hey, Captain. I heard back from the CSI assigned to the Jennings's case. She verified that the only prints on Audrey's personal items were Natalie's. I recommend we move forward with this as a kidnapping case."

Pausing momentarily to consider this as he got comfortable in his chair, Captain Reynolds replied, "I agree."

"Have we heard back on Audrey's laptop? I know the guys in Orlando should've gotten it by this morning."

"I haven't heard anything yet, but you'll be the first to know when I do."

Darryl slowly nodded. "Now that Audrey's cell phone has been processed, I plan to borrow it from the medical examiner's office. It may contain clues to who took her."

"I'll call the ME's office and have the phone brought to you. How did your interrogation with Ms. Anderson's ex-boyfriend go? Does he look good for the kidnapping?"

"The guy admitted he didn't have an alibi for the time Audrey went missing. It could be a way of throwing us off his scent, but Carl also mentioned going to one of Audrey's volleyball matches at the end of the school year. He said he saw a man who resembled Audrey staring at her."

"Could have been a family member of hers."

"True, but according to Carl the guy took off before the end of her game. I have the name of the high school where the match took place, so I'll reach out to see if they have any security tape of the gym or parking lot from that night."

Captain Reynolds picked up Audrey's case folder from the pile on his desk. "I agree Carl might be sending you off on a wild goose chase. Are you planning on questioning the parents to see if they're aware of a possible male look-alike of their daughter?"

"Yep. I have Audrey's parents coming in now to answer some more questions—that being one of them. I also want to let them know we plan on treating Audrey's disappearance as a kidnapping case."

"Sounds like you have everything under control, as usual. Just get me your report by the end of the day."

With the discussion over, Darryl walked out of his boss's office at the same time Audrey's parents were being led by an officer to one of the interview rooms.

Darryl collected his legal pad and pen from his desk before joining Mr. and Mrs. Jennings.

"Hi folks, thank you for coming in. I don't plan to keep you long. I gather you haven't received any ransom requests or anything of that nature?"

"No, we haven't received any calls, besides Natalie and Keith calling this morning to see how the investigation is going. Are we here because you agree Audrey has been kidnapped?" Mr. Jennings asked.

"Yes. We have evidence that leads us to believe Audrey has been kidnapped."

When Mrs. Jennings started to cry, Mr. Jennings wrapped his arm around her shoulders.

"Audrey's personal items, including her surfboard, were wiped clean of prints. If she had left the items in the church shrubs, chances are she wouldn't have seen the need to wipe them down."

"We already knew she was kidnapped. Our daughter would never leave us. She's our whole world," Mr. Jennings replied. After wiping away a single rogue tear, he asked, "Have you found any evidence as to who took Audrey?"

Darryl stared at his legal pad and contemplated whether it was worth asking about the look-alike at the volleyball game. Having no other leads, besides the ball-capped guy at the church parking lot, he decided he must. "We got a tip that a man resembling your daughter was at one of her last volleyball matches. Supposedly, the mystery man was overly interested in her throughout the match. It was back in mid-May. Is it possible a family member was there that night?"

The couple exchanged a glance before Mr. Jennings turned to Darryl. "We don't have any family in the area. Margaret and I don't have any living siblings, and no nieces or nephews. Both of our parents have passed. It couldn't be anyone we're related to—"

But before he could say anything else, Mrs. Jennings placed a hand on his arm. "Maybe not, but maybe it was someone Audrey is related to."

Puzzled by this last remark, Darryl looked back and forth between the couple, doing his best to process this statement. Then it became clear. "Audrey's not your biological child."

Mrs. Jennings took a deep breath. "Fifteen years into our marriage, we were told we couldn't have children. We agreed that adoption would allow us to give a child a loving home."

Mr. Jennings added, "At that point, I put in for a leave of absence from work, and we told our family and friends I had been transferred out of state for a year to help open a new investment firm branch. When we came back home, we introduced everyone to Audrey. No one knew she was adopted."

Mrs. Jennings continued, "We adopted Audrey from a young woman who didn't have the means to take care of her. And Audrey's biological father had passed away. We chose to adopt out of state so our family wouldn't find out. We didn't want to hear their objections about us adopting a baby or have them treat our child any differently because she wasn't blood."

"The adoption—it was a closed adoption then? There were no interactions between Audrey and her biological family over the years?" Darryl was a bit lost as to how a family member could've found her after all this time.

"Yes, it was a closed adoption. Not only did we not want anyone to know she was adopted, but her mother wanted to keep Audrey a secret from her family. She lived in a woman's shelter while she was pregnant and planned to move in with relatives after Audrey was born and the adoption paperwork was final," Mrs. Jennings explained.

"Did Audrey's mother have other kids? According to our witness, the man at the volleyball game was in his late twenties or early thirties. That means she would've had a son between the age of ten and fifteen years old back then."

Mr. Jennings replied, "No, that's not possible. Audrey's biological mother was only twenty-one years old when she was born. She wasn't old enough to have a son that age."

Darryl thought this over, then followed up with, "Could the biological father have had a son?"

"We weren't given any details about Audrey's biological father, just that he had died so he wouldn't be signing the adoption papers. His past wasn't disclosed to us," Mr. Jennings said.

"If it helps the case, we used an agency called Little Blessings Adoption Agency out of Chicago. It was in the same city as the women's shelter where Audrey's biological mother was staying," Mrs. Jennings said.

Darryl scribbled a note to remind himself to contact the agency for information on Audrey's family history. *Maybe there's record of older siblings on the father's side.* "You said you didn't want anyone to know Audrey was adopted. Did that include Audrey?"

The guilt written on the couple's faces was apparent.

After a long exhale, Mr. Jennings spoke up. "I know what you're thinking, but Audrey is everything to us. The thought of her learning the truth and wanting to have a relationship with her biological relatives is heartbreaking."

A tear rolled down Mrs. Jennings's face as she leaned into her husband for support. Mr. Jennings pulled her in close and continued to keep his arm around her when he faced the detective again.

"Just to verify, neither of you have ever been contacted by someone claiming to be related to Audrey or asking about her past. Is that correct? I need to know the truth."

Mr. Jennings replied, "No, never. They couldn't find us even if they wanted to. That was agreed upon by both parties."

"Do you remember what Audrey's biological mother's name is?"

It didn't take but a second for Mrs. Jennings to respond. "Yes, her name is Marissa Carter." Another tear ran down her cheek.

Realizing the couple had been through enough emotional trauma to last them a lifetime, Darryl decided to wrap up the conversation. "Mr. and Mrs. Jennings, thank you again for coming in. If you can think of anything else, please give me a call."

Once he had walked them out of the precinct's main entrance and saw them to their vehicle, Darryl circled back around to his boss's office. "I have a favor to ask."

Captain Reynolds turned from his computer screen. "Shoot."

Dropping into a chair, Darryl explained, "Mr. and Mrs. Jennings disclosed that Audrey was adopted. There may be truth to Carl's story regarding a male look-alike at Audrey's volleyball match. I might need a court order if the adoption agency won't give me access to the adoption file."

Captain Reynolds rested both elbows on his desk and folded his hands as he replied, "Contact the agency and see what you can find out before we have to jump through the hoops of getting a court order."

"I understand. I'll reach out right away and see what information they're willing to provide. But we're already past the twenty-four-hour mark in this case. My only other lead is the best friend's ex."

"Officers have already been to Carl's house with a search warrant. They didn't find anything, but we have an officer shadowing him in case Mr. Bennett is keeping Audrey in another location."

Darryl's shoulders noticeably relaxed.

Attempting to hide a yawn, he got up from the chair. Darryl was halfway through the doorway when Captain Reynolds said, "You haven't slept much since starting back last night. Reach out to the adoption agency, get me your report, then go home and get some rest."

Darryl agreed that rest would do him good. He thanked his boss and returned to his desk to search for the adoption agency's phone number.

# Chapter 14

There wasn't much in the room she could use to get an extensive workout, but Audrey made do with what she had. Using full bottles of water for arm weights, she simultaneously did her lunges while raising the full bottles above her head.

Since the concrete floor was too hard for her back, Audrey utilized the mattress to do her sit-ups. She decided to do fifty each day, at least until her belly was too large to do them anymore. The next part of her workout entailed a total of twenty-five each front and back leg kicks. She ended her routines with twenty-five jumping jacks and fifteen squats.

Quite a few hours had passed since her kidnapper turned the light on, and thankfully it hadn't been turned off yet.

A long line of ants had since emerged from a crack at the base of the wall in the corner behind her makeshift toilet. The little critters made their way to the half-eaten hot dog lying in the middle of the floor. Normally any kind of bug in her living space bothered Audrey, but there wasn't much to entertain her. So, she resolved to watch their efforts as they picked apart the hot dog bun and carried off tiny pieces into the wall.

Passing the time until the masked man returned, Audrey gazed down at the promise ring Keith gave her—the only jewelry she wore. She thought back on the night that resulted in her pregnancy.

\*\*\*

She and Keith had been on their way to a Fourth of July party hosted by a close high school friend. Keith had pulled up to their friend's house, and after turning off his truck, he reached into his glove compartment and pulled out a ring box.

"Audrey, you know how much you mean to me. I see a future for us—getting married someday and having a family together. We're still young and have college ahead of us. So I want to give you something that symbolizes my promise that no matter how far apart we are, you're the person I plan to spend the rest of my life with. I love you."

When he opened the ring box, there was a quarter-carat princess-cut diamond ring in a white gold band resting in it. Audrey didn't know what to say. She picked up the ring and read the engraving: *Keith and Audrey 4EVER.*

As tears clouded her vision, she smiled. "It's beautiful. I love you too and promise to love you for the rest of my life."

That night had not been their first act of lovemaking, but it would be the most memorable, especially for Audrey.

*** 

That promise had meant the world to her, but she had a bigger promise to keep now. While a baby may not have been in their plans, at least not at this point in their lives, the child was a result of their love, and that's all that mattered to her.

For the first time since finding out she was pregnant, Audrey pressed a hand to her abdomen and whispered her first words to her child. "You hear that? Even though you weren't planned, I love you more than words can say. I'll do whatever I can to get us home. I promise."

She lovingly patted her stomach as the locks on the door began to turn.

Audrey rose from the floor to get in position on the mattress. As usual, the masked man had a new plate of food and two more bottles of water with him.

*I can keep my other bottles for arm weights and drink these ones.* She watched him place the food away from the plate that was being scavenged by ants. The new plate contained a sandwich on whole wheat bread, a red apple, and a small, prepackaged bag of carrot sticks.

The stranger snatched the old plate. "Eat the food so they don't." He pointed to the bugs scurrying back toward the crack in the wall.

He turned to leave, but Audrey whispered, "Thank you for the light."

This stopped him in his tracks. He whipped back around and replied, "I didn't do it for you. I did it for that bastard you're carrying. Don't ever forget that."

Her hormones took control and Audrey lashed out. "If you're only doing it for the baby, then what were you planning to do to me before you found out I was pregnant?" She instantly regretted the question.

To her horror, he answered, "Not what I *was* going to do to you, but what I *will* do to you. That plan hasn't changed, just the timing of it has." With a wicked smile showing through his mask, he stomped out of the room, slamming the door behind him.

Taken aback by this response, Audrey sat on the mattress staring at the door. The sick feeling she had when she first awoke in this room was now much worse. Her head was spinning with so many possibilities of what he planned on doing to her.

*He must find pleasure in making me squirm. If he's that sadistic, then who knows what he's capable of.*

Audrey retrieved the food and bottles waters before returning to the mattress.

"I'm not going down without a fight," she said out loud, but her emotions got the best of her. Tears streamed down her cheeks. She took a bite of the sandwich, hoping it would lessen the nausea. If she was going to get out of here alive, she couldn't let him get into her head. Her child deserved to meet his father and know how wonderful his grandparents were.

That meant she needed to not only survive her kidnapping but thrive in order to take down her captor.

# Chapter 15

Darryl had called the adoption agency before leaving the precinct on Saturday evening but got their voice mail. The female voice on the recording stated the office was closed for the weekend and would open again at eight o'clock Monday morning.

Darryl had left his name, phone number, and a brief message.

When he got back to the station on Sunday morning, he spent the whole day searching the precinct's law enforcement database for information on Audrey's biological mother, Marissa Carter. His original search had brought up twenty-two Marissa Carters in the Chicago area.

By the time Darryl narrowed this list down to the Marissa Carter who stayed at a woman's shelter at the time of Audrey's birth, it was five minutes to ten. Soon after, the search came to a screeching halt when the only phone numbers listed for her were either no longer in service or had been recycled. Even if he could locate a good number for Audrey's mother, Darryl didn't want to make the call that late at night.

By seven o'clock Monday morning, Darryl returned to work eager to hear back from the adoption agency.

Strolling up to his desk, he spotted a note requesting that he see Cathy.

Darryl quickly reached the lobby, hopeful to get some good news. "Good morning. I believe you have something for me," he said, beaming.

She looked up from her computer monitor with a smile of her own. Brushing aside her gray bangs that were getting into her eyes, she said, "Sure do. Shortly before you came in this morning, Mel from the medical examiner's office dropped off a phone for you. I signed for it so you better not lose it." She winked at him as she handed it over.

Darryl thanked her and carried the phone, sealed in a clear plastic bag, back to his desk.

Since Audrey's laptop hadn't come back from Orlando yet, he hoped to find something on her cell phone. Hopefully a clue as to why she had been acting so odd around her family and friends.

He ripped open the bag and immediately turned on the phone. When the first screen popped up, it confirmed his assumption: The phone had password protection.

Praying he didn't have to send it to the forensics examiner to be unlocked, he pulled out his legal pad from his desk drawer and skimmed the pages as he hunted for Mrs. Jennings's number. Finding it, he reached for his phone and noticed the flashing light.

The only voice message began, "Detective Harris, this is Keith Lennox, Audrey's boyfriend. I called and spoke with Mr. and Mrs. Jennings last night, and they said they haven't heard anything since talking to you on Saturday. I was wondering if you had some new information by now or maybe even a lead. Please give me a call when you have time."

The sadness in Keith's voice was not lost on Darryl. And even though he found out something major about Audrey from her parents, it wasn't Darryl's place to tell her boyfriend. If her kidnapping had anything to do with her being adopted, then the news would come out eventually. He wrote himself a quick note to call Keith back after contacting Mrs. Jennings.

As he took a sip of the coffee he poured himself when he first arrived at the station, he dialed the home phone number.

"Hello," Mrs. Jennings cautiously answered.

"Good morning. This is Detective Harris. I apologize for calling so early, but I'm hoping you can help me with something,"

"Of course, whatever you need."

"Audrey's cell phone has been processed for evidence and is now in my possession. But I can't get into it because of the password protection. I know we didn't have luck with her laptop, but by chance do you happen to know the password to her cell phone?"

"Well, let's see. It used to be her birthday, October 2, 1998, or 10021998."

Darryl immediately entered the sequence of numbers into the cell phone, and to his amazement, it unlocked. *How many secrets can her cell phone hold if her mother knows the password?* "Thank you, Mrs. Jennings. That worked."

"I'm glad. Also, Natalie and Keith keep calling and asking if they can help in the search for Audrey. They both decided to hold off on going to college right now so they're available if you need them."

"That's good to know. I may have some information for you soon. We're working a few different leads right now. But I'll notify you once I hear something."

"I'll let Daniel, Natalie, and Keith know that as well."

They said their good-byes and hung up.

Searching the browser history on the cell phone, Darryl noticed Audrey most recently pulled up Gainesville apartments, Gainesville jobs, and Gainesville day care centers. This last one seemed strange. *Her mother said she was accepted to the University of Florida in Gainesville, so the apartment search and even the job search for that area seem normal. But why was she searching for day cares?*

As he scrolled down past a few more random search results, he found his answer. The next search items included: pregnancy symptoms at six weeks, how long morning sickness lasts, and maternity clothes. Now he knew why Audrey was acting out of character. *She was pregnant! So why didn't she tell anyone . . . or had she?*

Darryl located Keith's cell phone number and dialed it.

"Hi, this is Keith."

"Hi, Detective Harris here calling you back."

"Yes. Have you heard anything about Audrey?"

"We're working some leads and anticipate having news for you soon. I just spoke with Mrs. Jennings and told her the same thing. I actually have some questions for you if you have time to stop by the precinct this morning."

"I can come in now if that works for you."

"Perfect. See you soon."

Once he was off the phone, Darryl moseyed over to the kitchen to get another cup of coffee and grab something to eat for breakfast. Spotting a box of bagels, he picked the healthiest one he could find—a sliced blueberry multigrain bagel—and spread a generous layer of cream cheese on each half. After pouring himself fresh coffee, he went back to his desk to go over the text messages on Audrey's cell phone.

Taking a bite of his bagel, he began his search with the most recent messages. It didn't take long for him to see that Audrey had been dodging her boyfriend and best friend for the last few weeks. *It must've been hard on her to know she was pregnant and not tell anyone.*

Darryl read through three months of text messages before moving on to her emails. But after going through the last six months of those messages, nothing stuck out as suspicious.

As he ate the rest of his bagel, he sat back in his chair and wondered, *Could this news have anything to do with her disappearance? Did she run away so no one would know she was pregnant?* That didn't line up with her personal items being wiped clean of prints or the fact that she was searching for day cares in the same city she was supposed to attend college in a couple of weeks. *No, but this would explain her recent change in behavior though.*

At this point, he hadn't ruled out the Cocoa Beach Killer. It had been close to two years since they found the last victim's body, but a sick psychopath like this guy didn't stop what he felt the need to do. If he was involved in Audrey's disappearance, then there must be a reason he was dormant for this long. *Maybe he was picked up on lesser charges and got out of jail recently, or maybe he relocated to another city or state where the cases haven't been linked.*

For Audrey's sake, Darryl hoped his serial killer wasn't involved. No matter how much he wanted to catch that evil bastard and bring him to justice, he didn't want to see another girl victimized like that.

In the meantime, there was nothing developing with the lead on Carl Bennett. If Carl was telling the truth about the spectator at the volleyball match, then Darryl needed to find out if and how that individual knew Audrey. *Could they somehow be related? If so, why did he leave the game early without saying good-bye?*

He pulled up the high school's phone number online and dialed it. There was ringing on the other end of the line until it went to the principal's voice mail. Even though it was summer break, the principal still worked office hours. Darryl left a message asking him to call back right away.

After hanging up, Darryl continued his search for the biological mother's contact information. Or at least until Keith showed up, at which point Darryl planned to confirm his suspicions concerning Audrey's pregnancy.

# Chapter 16

Audrey awoke to the bright light above her and the locks as they turned. She assumed it was Monday morning, because for the past two days she noticed the lightbulb went out for a long period of time each day and came back on when her kidnapper returned with food.

She had started scraping the wall behind her pillow with small lines to indicate how many days she had been in this room—in case she was unfortunate to be stuck here long term.

*Another similarity to being in jail.*

The stranger emerged with the same rope and blindfold.

*Must be time for another shower.* She hated the thought of being nude in front of her kidnapper, but this time she was determined to get a good look at her surroundings and see if there was anyone living or working nearby.

"Get up," he demanded as he approached her.

She gradually stood up and held out her wrists.

With the rope and blindfold in place, they exited through the narrow hallway into the sunlight. Her assumption about it being morning seemed to be accurate.

While it was warm out, it wasn't as hot as a typical August afternoon.

When her blindfold was removed, she found herself in the same spot as last time. As the masked man untied her wrists, Audrey scanned the area to see what was past the shower.

Since her kidnapper had her standing close to the structure, she could barely see past its concrete walls. But when she did get a peek around the corner, her heart sank. There was nothing but grass and fencing for what appeared to be miles. *Where am I? He brought me out to the middle of nowhere!*

"Get in the shower. There's another dress for you to wear so leave the one you have on in there."

Audrey noticed her shorts, tank top, and bathing suit were no longer in the shower. *What did he do with them?*

"What are you waiting for? Get going or I'll remove your clothes and wash you myself."

Audrey inched her way over to the shower. With the water running, she kept her back to the masked man and stepped sideways under the stream.

Outside of her daily exercises in the room, she didn't do much to need this shower. *If only the pervert would put up a shower curtain, but then he's probably smarter than he looks.* She would certainly find a way to escape if she was given just one moment's head start.

When she turned the water off, she immediately pulled the towel off the ledge. Drying off in record time, she snatched the dress. *No underwear.* As she pretended to casually towel dry her hair, she turned around to look past the stranger in the direction of where they came from.

The concrete shower was butted up against the building they exited from, which backed up to a large, wooded area. *Okay, that might be my escape route.*

It wasn't ideal, but at least she wouldn't be attempting to run away out in the open—like the rest of the property on the other side of the shower.

It didn't take him long to notice Audrey wasn't looking directly at him. He rushed toward her and shoved the blindfold over her eyes before he grabbed the towel from her and threw it on the ground. Then, with heavy, agitated breathing, he bound the rope around her wrists so tight it cut into her skin.

She didn't let him see her pain, even though she could feel the hate he had for her. It was as if he wanted to do so much more, but the baby was in his way.

*Does he truly care about my baby, or does he want to sell him or her to the highest bidder? Is that what this is all about? Does he want to earn some extra money before he does whatever he wants with me?* The possibilities were blood-chilling.

Before she could think about it any longer, he took her roughly by her upper arm and led her back inside.

Hastily making their way back down the hallway, he shoved her into a sitting position on the mattress. After untying her and whipping the blindfold off, he glared down at her.

Now she felt both ill and terrified at what he might be contemplating.

"You think you're so smart, don't you? I can see you're thinking of ways to escape, but I promise you something: If you try to get away like you did the first time, I'll make you regret it. Don't think just because I bring you food and water and let you have showers and light in your room that I care one shit about you."

He said this with such loathing she was petrified he would kill her right here and now.

"Do you understand me?!"

Not wanting to fuel the fire in him any more than she had, Audrey quietly replied. "Yes, I understand."

He continued to stare at her for another minute as if he was gauging her sincerity, but then he started to leave the room. Before he got to the door, he collected the empty plate and water bottles. Seeing the wide-eyed expression on her face, he seemed satisfied with his scare tactic. He locked the door behind him.

Audrey sat on the mattress for a while thinking back on his hateful speech.

Then the door began to unlock again. He returned with another plate. This time it contained scrambled eggs, wheat toast, and a container of strawberry yogurt. He placed the two bottles of water he was holding between his forearm and rib cage onto the ground beside the plate. As usual, there were no utensils, making this meal more difficult than it should be to eat. He wasn't going to hear her complain though—not after what he threatened.

As if reading her mind, he glanced up and gave her a sadistic smile before he left her again.

Feeling confident he wouldn't be back any time soon, Audrey pulled out the comb he threw at her the last time she had taken a shower. She began to slowly work through the tangles in her hair.

*Does he realize I still have this?* She sincerely hoped not. If he wanted her to feel like she was in prison, then she would act like it. *There must be a way of turning the comb into a weapon to be used against him.*

However, she needed to first make sure the comb wasn't on his radar. Any element of surprise she could gain, Audrey planned to take advantage of. But she would also have to choose her timing wisely in case she only got one shot at escaping.

# Chapter 17

Darryl continued his search for a current phone number or address for Audrey's biological mother. If he could locate her on his own, then he wouldn't have to rely on the adoption agency or get a court order to obtain the information.

He looked up in time to see Audrey's boyfriend, Keith, walking toward him from the lobby.

"Is this a good time?"

"Of course. Let's find a room for some privacy." Darryl got up and led Keith to one of the available interview rooms. "Do you want anything to drink?"

"No, I'm good."

Once the door was closed behind them, they each took a seat.

"I appreciate you coming in. Something's come up, and I want to see if you are aware of it."

Keith's legs started bobbing up and down, while his hands gripped the arms of his chair.

"I was able to go through the Internet search history on Audrey's cell phone."

The boyfriend continued to stare at him as if he was on the edge of his seat.

"Audrey had been looking up apartments and job opportunities in the Gainesville area. Were you aware of this?"

Keith shrugged. "Audrey is supposed to start college in Gainesville in a couple of weeks. It makes sense she wants to work a part-time job in between classes. But I thought she was going to live in a dorm for the first year or two that she's there."

Darryl had a feeling this kid didn't know where his questions were leading. "Keith, you mentioned the other day that Audrey hasn't been herself recently, and you thought she might be breaking things off with you before she goes off to college. Could there have been any other reason for her odd behavior? Anything at all that you can think of?"

Keith's eyebrows turned in as he stared down at the table. When he returned his attention to Darryl, he said, "No, I have no idea."

"Is there a chance Audrey could be pregnant?"

Keith's jaw dropped.

"Audrey's search history brought up a lot of questions a woman who's pregnant might ask."

Guilt washed over Keith's face, and he finally responded, "Yes, I guess so. We were always careful, but the night of the Fourth of July party . . ." he paused to take a breath and continued sheepishly, ". . . the condom broke. When I realized what happened, it was already too late. I didn't tell Audrey, because I figured the chances of her getting pregnant that one time were slim. If she did get pregnant, I thought she'd tell me, and we'd decide what to do next."

Darryl slowly nodded.

"She never said anything, and that was over a month ago. But then that explains why she's been so distant. Maybe that was what she was going to tell me at dinner the other night."

"I'm not a hundred percent sure, but it does appear that way. I'm sorry you had to find out like this. Would Audrey have made the decision to abort the child and that's why she disappeared?"

Keith sat up straighter and responded assertively. "Never. Audrey would never do that. If she's pregnant, she'll do everything in her power to protect that child. If she knows she's pregnant, then we have a better chance at getting her back home alive. I know it."

Darryl sincerely hoped what the young man was saying was true.

"Detective, can we keep Audrey's possible pregnancy between us? I mean, I don't see the need to say anything to Mr. and Mrs. Jennings at this point. It'll only upset them more."

Darryl didn't see the harm in this request. "That may be wise. Her parents already have enough to worry about."

Having run out of questions for Keith, the detective escorted the young man to the front entrance. "We're following multiple leads at this time. Don't give up hope. If what you say is true, then your girlfriend has a lot to live for."

Keith nodded then shuffled out of the precinct.

Back at his desk, Darryl saw the flashing light on his phone. He pulled up the voice message.

"Detective Harris, this is Ronald Camp, the principal at Melbourne High School. You said you need security tape footage of our gym from back in May. I have a call into our security company to see if they have the footage archived, or if it's already been erased. They only hold film for so long, but I hope to give you good news when I hear back from them. I'll talk to you soon," the principal finished before the message ended.

*Well, there's still a possibility I'll be able to prove Carl's story about Audrey's secret admirer to be true. And if not, I'll have more reason to focus my efforts on Carl as the prime suspect.*

"Harris, meet me in my office," Captain Reynolds ordered as he passed Darryl's desk.

"Do you have some good news for me?" Darryl asked as he trailed his boss into the office and sat down.

"I may. I got a call from Officer Brown. He's gone over the security footage of the Methodist church where the Jennings's girl went missing. He also reviewed the security footage from one of the stores in the nearby shopping plaza. He has the footage cued up to the time around Audrey's disappearance. I told him you'd be over shortly to go over it. Make sure I get a report of your findings."

"Of course!" Darryl shouted as he rushed out the door. He hurried down the corridor lined with offices on both sides. When he opened the door to the IT department, he immediately caught the officer's attention.

"Hey, Darryl. That was quick. Thought I had time to go have lunch before you came by," Officer Joe Brown joked.

"Don't let me keep you from a meal, Joe," Darryl teased in response to the overweight officer. They had worked on many cases together so their relationship had grown to an exchange of lighthearted banter and the use of first names.

"Very funny. Well, there isn't much to see on the church's security tape, but I found something fishy on the thrift store footage. It's cued to where I believe your culprit comes into view," Joe explained as Darryl planted himself in the seat next to him and leaned forward to see the screen better.

Joe played the footage just as a white van pulled up to the store. The security camera faced out to the parking lot where the van was parked—in front of the sidewalk that connected the coffee shop, pet store, and thrift store.

Darryl noted the time on the date stamp in the right corner of the screen. It was from eleven forty-five the morning Audrey went missing.

"Watch as the driver gets out of the van and goes around to the side of the vehicle. He keeps his head down, and since he's wearing a ball cap, you can't get a good glimpse of his face."

Darryl noted that the surfer's recollection of the guy was pretty accurate. He looked to be about six feet two inches tall and probably a good two hundred thirty pounds, most of which appeared to be muscle.

The driver pulled back the side door of the van. Darryl said, "He has an oversized black plastic tub with wheels."

"Yeah, and at first, I thought he was donating items in it to the thrift store, but that's not the case. You see how he walked away, wheeling the tub out of range of the camera? Now watch this." Joe fast forwarded the tape to approximately an hour and a half later.

When the tape stopped, Darryl noted with curiosity, "He's rolling the tub back to the van, but he's having a difficult time getting it into the vehicle compared to when he took it out."

"Yep."

A sinking feeling hit his gut. "Audrey's in that plastic tub. But the surfer never mentioned the guy in the ball cap having a tub with him."

Joe rubbed his chin absent-mindedly.

Darryl continued to consider this while he and Joe stared at the monitor.

Then Darryl suddenly sat up. "I think I know how he did it—how he kidnapped Audrey without anyone seeing. He was hiding on the west side of the church where the parking lot and main entrance are located. That goes along with what the surfer said about him walking out of sight. You can't see that side of the church from the road. And there's an overhang that provides plenty of shade on the walkway. He must've stayed under its shadow when Audrey came around the corner."

Darryl shifted in his seat before continuing. "At that point, he snuck up behind her, rendered her unconscious, and placed her in the tub. It would've taken him only a few minutes to do all that and wipe her personal items down before throwing them into the shrubs."

Then his eyes narrowed in on the screen. "But was she alive when he put her in the tub?"

Joe rewound the tape and hit play. "See how he put the tub into the van—carefully—even though it's obviously heavy?"

"Wait, zoom in right there." Darryl pointed to the tub. "There are holes along the top, just below the lid."

Joe squinted as he focused on the image on the screen. "You're right. And the scrubs he's wearing might mean he works at a hospital or doctor's office of some sort where he has access to medications to knock someone out."

"You said there isn't much to see on the church's security tape. Can you get a glimpse of the guy with the ball cap at any point during the time when he walked away from the thrift store and before he returns?"

Joe shook his head. "The security cameras only cover a few feet in front of the main entrance of the church. Your guy either knew that or got lucky, because he isn't in any of the security footage. Even the van's license plate can't be seen by the thrift store's camera. It seems he had everything planned out, like he was waiting for that specific opportunity."

"I suppose that's a commonly owned van too," Darryl said sarcastically.

Joe slowly nodded. "It is. My search resulted in a list of over forty vans of that make, model, and color within a twenty-five-mile radius."

While Darryl was thinking of ways to shrink this list down to the van he saw on the tape, Joe hesitantly asked, "Do you think this could be the same guy? The Cocoa Beach Killer case you've been investigating all these years?"

Not surprised by this question, especially since the case was always on his mind, Darryl answered, "It's possible. This is the closest we've gotten to him if it is. Unfortunately, it's too soon to know. We need to find something on that van that stands out if we're going to ID this guy."

# Chapter 18

After leaving Joe with the daunting task of reducing the list of van owners in the area down to their ball-capped suspect, Darryl stopped by his desk before going to lunch. The light was flashing on his phone so he pulled up his message.

"Hi, detective. This is Mel. I'm checking in to make sure you received Audrey Jennings's cell phone. Also, you should've received a copy of the report on the evidence, or lack thereof, on her personal items. Okay, that's it. Have a good day."

*Do I sense a hint of nervousness in Mel's voice?*

Since the medical examiner's office that Mel worked out of was in the building next to the precinct, Darryl decided he'd stop by to see her on his way to lunch. He located his car key in his desk drawer and strolled out of the precinct.

It was another hot day in August, with temperatures reaching a high of 103 degrees and humidity at almost one hundred percent. Darryl wiped away a bead of sweat from his brow as he walked into the building's main entrance.

"Good afternoon. I would like to see Mel Crosby if she's available," he said to the desk clerk.

The young woman smiled at the good-looking detective. "Sure, let me give her a quick call."

"Thanks." He took a seat near the glass doors.

"You're in luck. Mel is here. She's about to go to lunch so she'll be right out."

Darryl gave the blonde a friendly smile. "Sounds good."

While peering out the glass doors, he heard Mel step through the walkway. "Hello. You must've gotten my voice message. I hope the cell phone provided more evidence than Audrey's other personal items."

Even though she was half-joking, Mel's eyebrows were raised as she waited his response.

Standing to his feet, Darryl had a large grin on his face. "Yes, thanks for that. I heard you were going to lunch. Care to join me so we can discuss the cell phone and other developments in the case?" He held his breath, unsure how she would respond.

Mel didn't say anything for a few moments, making him think she was coming up with an excuse not to go with him. "Sure, that'd be nice. As long as we can eat inside, because it's way too hot out," she said with a chuckle.

Seeing her beautiful smile made his insides buzz.

After a five-minute ride up the road, it didn't take long for them to get a booth toward the back of the Mexican restaurant.

"So, did you get into Audrey's cell phone yet?"

"I did. Her mother had the password. I was surprised. I figured it meant there wouldn't be anything useful on it. But I was able to find out the secret she was keeping from her family and friends. At least I'm ninety percent sure it's the reason for her change in behavior."

Mel gazed at him intently.

"She might be pregnant."

Mel looked stunned but recovered from the news quickly. "Wow, that couldn't have been planned since she just graduated from high school. None of her family or friends knew?" Mel lifted a finger to signal the waitress who then walked over to greet them.

Pulling out her notepad from the front of her apron, the waitress asked, "Good afternoon. What can I get you folks to drink?"

"I'll have a water, and if my friend is ready to order lunch, I know what I'm having." Mel winked at Darryl.

"Yes, I am. Go ahead." He smiled at her.

"I'll take the chicken quesadilla lunch special please, with guacamole on the side."

"And I'll have a sweet tea and three ground beef tacos a la carte, and a chicken quesadilla as well," Darryl said.

They handed their menus to the waitress at the same time.

Once the waitress moved on to another table, Darryl finally responded to Mel's question. "I only brought it up to the boyfriend. It seems he didn't know. He thought Audrey was going to break up with him, because they were accepted to colleges in different states."

"His girlfriend goes missing and days later he finds out she's carrying his child. That must've been a rough conversation."

"Keith was shook up about it, but he was also concerned about her parents finding out." Darryl couldn't take his eyes off of Mel. *I hope she doesn't pick up on my feelings for her if she doesn't feel the same way about me.*

"I'm sorry," he blurted out, and before he could stop himself, he added, "I shouldn't have left you that morning without saying anything."

Mel's eyes held steady on his without any indication of what she was thinking. A few moments passed before she replied. "Thanks. I was a bit stunned, but I wasn't expecting anything more from that night. I had recently gotten out of a long-term relationship, and you were going through a divorce. Guess we were each other's rebounds."

He mulled over her response. He wasn't sure if he was happy she held no hard feelings toward him, or disappointed that she didn't.

"That's good to know after all this time. I figured you'd be upset with me for not calling you after I left that

morning. Some women might've felt abandoned or used."
He waited to see if this comment helped uncover her true
feelings, if she was holding them back.

"I once thought there could be more between us than
just one night. We always work well together and have a
lot in common. But sometimes things don't work out the
way you want them to, and you have to move on."

The waitress returned and placed their drinks and
meals in front of them.

Since Darryl didn't know what to say next, he started
in on his tacos. It wasn't exactly what he was expecting
when he invited her out to lunch, but he didn't deserve
her undying love either.

They continued to eat in silence. When they finished,
Darryl paid for both their lunches. Mel tried to insist she
pay for her own lunch, but he won out with, "Consider it
the rest of my apology."

She laughed when he followed this up with his
winning smile.

*Maybe lunch together wasn't a bad idea after all.*

When he had returned Mel back to the medical
examiner's office and made his way to the precinct's
kitchen for his third cup of coffee, Darryl got a call on his
cell phone.

"This is Detective Harris."

"Hi, my name is Lisa Campbell. I'm one of the
adoption lawyers here at the Little Blessings Adoption

Agency in Chicago. You left your work number and your cell phone number on the agency's voice mail."

"Yes, of course. As I mentioned on the voice message, I'm hoping to gain some information on an adoption. The individual who was adopted is Audrey Jennings, and she was adopted by Daniel and Margaret Jennings. Unfortunately, Audrey went missing three days ago, and we have reason to believe a blood relative was trying to contact her before her disappearance."

"I'm very sorry. That's awful. But being in law enforcement, you can understand I can't release closed adoption files without a court order. If you can obtain one, then I'll be happy to be of assistance. However, if I can be honest with you, I find it hard to believe a blood relative could find someone who had a closed adoption."

"A witness recently saw a man who shares the same physical features as the young lady. And now that she's missing, I don't think it's a coincidence," he countered with obvious agitation in his voice.

"I'm sorry I can't be of more assistance. My hands are tied."

Sensing the conversation was going nowhere without the court documents the agency was requiring, Darryl thanked Ms. Campbell for her time. Then he assured her he would be talking to her soon.

With his cell phone back on his belt clip, Darryl marched into his boss's office. Without waiting for

Captain Reynolds to look up from the document he was reading, Darryl interrupted. "I just heard back from the adoption agency in the Audrey Jennings's case. They're not going to provide any information until we get a court order."

"Then it's a good thing I already put in a request for one," his Captain confidently replied. "I talked to the assistant DA, and all he needs is the adoptive parents to sign a consent form to have the adoption file released to our office. Mr. and Mrs. Jennings came in earlier when you were at lunch and signed everything. I already had an officer bring the signed documents over to the assistant DA to obtain the court order from a judge. We'll have it sometime today or tomorrow morning."

"You're the best, and you apparently know it," Darryl teased his boss while sporting a grin. He then went on to describe what he and Officer Brown found on the thrift store security tape.

Captain Reynolds steepled his hands in front of his face as he listened.

"There's no way of verifying from the tape that Audrey was in the tub, but the timing seems to indicate he knocked her out and used the tub to move her. Officer Brown is searching through the footage for clues to identify the mystery man or the van he used," Darryl said.

"It sounds like the best friend's ex is no longer our prime suspect. Verify Carl Bennett doesn't own a van of the same make and model. If that's the case, I can pull back the shadow we have on him."

"Will do. And let me know as soon as you hear back on the court order." Darryl hoped the adoption file would provide the lead he urgently needed.

# Chapter 19

The light flickered on above her indicating it was morning again. Audrey sat up on the mattress and made sure her dress covered her in the right places. It was apparently purchased at a thrift store or a garage sale, because it wasn't in the best shape. The purple was faded, and the hem was fraying badly.

*At least it has more material than the other dress he left for me.* There were short sleeves on this dress, and the length of it went past her knees. And since she didn't have undergarments, the dress's length was especially important to her.

The door swung open as the stranger carried in her breakfast. There was no change in his usual attire, except he was back in scrubs rather than the dark shirt and jeans.

He looked down at the empty plate. The two slices of cheese pizza and French fries were only slightly warm when he brought them to her last night. However, since she hadn't eaten since early morning, she had devoured them.

Audrey figured he must have been furious with her for looking around the property after she had finished her shower yesterday. The fact he brought her any more food that day only proved he didn't want to deny her child crucial nutrients.

"Must've been hungry last night," he snickered.

Audrey wasn't amused. Instead, she ignored him and peeked at the plate of food in his hand. She spotted a pill sitting amongst the oatmeal, assorted fruit, and bacon.

"What's the pill for?"

"It's a vitamin. Take it."

*It must be a prenatal vitamin for the baby. He must be expecting a big payday from selling my baby if he's going to the trouble of buying prenatal vitamins. Isn't he concerned that someone would question why a guy is buying used dresses or why he's purchasing prenatal vitamins?* She prayed somebody would notice something peculiar in his behavior soon so she could be rescued from this prison.

After taking the empty plate, he turned to glare at her.

Something about the heat in his eyes made her hair stand on end. He walked slowly toward her and extended his hand. When she stared at his hand with a questioning look, he followed this gesture with, "Give me the comb. I don't trust you with anything you can use against me."

Her heart plummeted in her chest. *So, he does remember it.* While maintaining eye contact, Audrey reached under her pillow and deposited the comb into his calloused hand. It was then that she realized he wasn't wearing gloves. The black ski mask was covering his face, but he either didn't see the need for the gloves or he had completely forgotten about them.

His penetrating eyes made her queasy.

"You might be more work than it's worth. If I even think you're planning to escape, I'll make sure your legs aren't able to get you anywhere, let alone out of this room."

Audrey didn't doubt his threat.

After another long, uncomfortable moment under his watchful eye, the stranger turned away. He collected the bucket from the corner before leaving.

When he was finished locking the door, Audrey exhaled. She didn't know for how long she had been holding her breath, but her heart was still racing. *How long until he gives in to his urges? It's obvious he's getting anxious to follow through with his original plans, whatever they are.*

Lying back down on the mattress, Audrey waited for the nausea to subside and her nerves to calm. *That was a close call.* He seemed to know her every move, and it was heartbreaking. *How am I going to get out of this room and away from that man if I can't outsmart him?*

She struggled to stop the emotions that were taking over. *What the hell does he plan to do to me and what does he want with my baby?*

She allowed herself to cry for a short while before forcing herself off the mattress and over to the plate of food. Choosing a strawberry first, she slowly ate it, then moved on to the remaining strawberries and green grapes. The three slices of bacon were burnt, but she managed to choke them down. Since there were no utensils, she didn't even try to eat the oatmeal. *It doesn't look appetizing anyway.*

Audrey took the pill off the plate and grabbed one of the bottles of water she left next to her mattress. The pill appeared larger than most vitamins she had taken so she wondered if it was safe to swallow.

*If he wanted to poison me, he could've done it with the food*, she rationalized. With that logic, she popped the pill into her mouth and washed it down with the water.

With nothing else to do, Audrey began her exercise routine. Since she had limited things to pass her time, she exercised multiple times a day. Watching the ants come and go pretty much made up the rest of her pathetic day. There wasn't anything left from her meal last night for the little creatures to eat, but the oatmeal would be plenty to draw them out of the wall.

When she had completed her exercises and drank the other half of her bottled water, Audrey marked the wall behind her pillow with a line to represent another day. She no longer had the comb so she used her longest fingernail to carve out just a slight indentation in the concrete wall. The simple task took much longer now, but it wasn't like she had anything better to do.

Audrey sat back against the wall as she heard the locks turn.

The door opened wide, and the stranger dropped the now empty bucket into its corner. "We're going outside for a few minutes. Put on your shoes." He pulled out the blindfold.

*Where are we going that I need shoes?*

With her shoes and blindfold on, he escorted her out of the room. There was no rope tied around her wrists. *Does he think I'm too scared to run if I'm given the opportunity? If so, he doesn't know me as well as he thinks.*

They exited the building and walked a good distance. It must've been at least an eighth of a mile—not too far, but in flip flops it felt like a lot.

Audrey figured it was at least mid-morning because the heat was increasing. The humidity was dreadful as usual in Florida in the summer. Suddenly, Audrey felt a wave of relief at the realization she was still in Florida.

"Sit and stay put." He pushed her into a lawn chair.

They were still outside because she could feel the sun beating down on her. But the sound of chains made her shudder. Then came the handcuffs placed around her wrists, which were attached to the chains. Audrey assumed the chains were anchored to something, since she could no longer move her arms away from her sides.

The chair sat so low that her fingertips were touching the ground.

*Why is he chaining me to a chair this far away from the building?* Her anxiety increased.

"Don't move an inch. I'll be watching you. If I see you try anything, this'll be the last time you leave the room. Do you understand me?"

"Yes."

Hearing his footsteps getting quieter as he got farther away, Audrey wondered if she was out here for some sick game of his, or if this was a way for her to get sunlight and fresh air. If it was the latter, then she knew better than to believe it was for *her* well-being. Anything he did was for the sake of the baby. But she was grateful for the time outside anyway.

Her thoughts were disrupted by noise off in the distance in front of her. Unsure if he was looking her way, Audrey didn't dare attempt to remove the blindfold.

*What's that sound?* Something large was coming closer to her. She could hear hooves hitting the ground. She listened closely to see if she recognized the animal making the noise.

"Here you go," came the barely audible words of the stranger from not too far off. The response he got in return was a horse's nicker.

*That's why there's so much land around here. He owns horses. Maybe that's why he wears jeans at times, even in the extreme temperatures of summer. But why the scrubs?*

Feeling the heat from the sun, she let her mind wander to a happier time—the first time she and Keith went to the beach together.

It was their first date, and they had gone to surf and play beach volleyball with two other young couples.

A volleyball net set up in front of one of the beach resorts was available to the public. Audrey's parents had only allowed her to go out for a few hours that day, but she had a blast. Both her and Keith's competitive spirits were uncovered that day when they played boys versus girls in the first match. The score had stayed tight with the girls winning the game by a single point.

She could tell right away Keith didn't like losing, but he was a good sport about it.

*I miss him.*

About twenty minutes later, the stranger was back to take the handcuffs off. The chains fell to the ground. Taking her by the arm, he led her in the direction they came from.

She was now confident this was just a means of giving her some much-needed sunlight and fresh air—for the baby.

*Will he make this a routine? If so, it'll not only give me a distraction during the day, but also a chance to make my escape.*

# Chapter 20

Darryl was back at the precinct around nine o'clock Tuesday morning. Four days after Audrey Jennings had gone missing.

With so many moving pieces to this investigation, he had been at the station late again last night. He had been putting together a report of his recent findings while struggling to locate contact information for Audrey's biological mother.

He slipped into the kitchen to pour himself a cup of coffee and find something to eat. But there was nothing but day-old bagels, so Darryl poured himself a cup of coffee and proceeded to his desk to check his voice messages.

"Harris, can you stop by my office?" Captain Reynolds's loud request echoed through the station.

Darryl took a detour in that direction. "Good morning."

Captain Reynolds gave him a half smile. "It is a good morning. I have two pieces of good news—and unfortunately one piece of bad news regarding the Jennings's case."

With his interest aroused, Darryl said, "Go ahead with the bad news first."

"Ronald Camp, principal of Melbourne High School, called the front desk. He had lost your direct number. Anyway, he said the company they use for their security cameras verified the footage from back in May was erased."

Seeing Darryl's shoulders slump, he continued. "But the court order came through this morning. It's been forwarded on to the Little Blessings Adoption Agency via email so we should be getting Ms. Jennings's adoption file soon."

"That is good news. And the second piece of good news?"

"The girl's laptop came in from Orlando this morning. Officer Brown is currently inspecting the files on it. You can meet with him when you're settled in."

After thanking his boss for the information, Darryl returned to his desk to get his pad and pen. Then he made his way toward the IT department to see his friend Joe.

Joe greeted him with a wide grin. "Good morning. I see you've heard the good news. I've been looking through Ms. Jennings's laptop for the last hour and nothing looks out of sorts."

Darryl took the empty seat next to Joe's. He took a sip of his now semi-warm coffee. "What have you found on it so far?"

"There are lots of pictures of what appear to be a boyfriend and pictures of friends and possibly family

144

members. There are also quite a few school papers and projects saved on it. I'm about to look through the Internet search history if you're interested."

"Yeah, sounds good." Darryl sat forward in his chair as his foot started to tap the floor vigorously.

Joe pulled up the Internet browser with a few clicks. Starting from the top, the search results included: OBGYN in Cocoa Beach, best vitamins to take when pregnant, and maternity clothes.

Passing a few more older search results on the list, one caught Darryl's eye—Adoption. Since there were no other details associated with this search, he wondered if Audrey was looking to give her child up for adoption or if she found out about her own adoption.

"Can you pull up when the search for adoption took place?"

The details came up within seconds. Joe replied, "Back in late July—July 25th to be exact. Why? Do you think this has something to do with her disappearance?"

Darryl took a moment to do the calculation in his head. "I'm not sure. If it had been weeks earlier, I'd say it was possible Audrey had discovered she was adopted, and therefore was looking for her biological parents. However, I have reason to believe she's pregnant. If her boyfriend is correct about the conception date, she could've known about the pregnancy and been looking into her options."

*Things can't be simple in this case, can they?*

Darryl asked, "Have you found anything on the ball-capped guy or his van from the thrift store's security footage?"

"No, not yet. I'm still going through the list of vans in the area and eliminating the ones that couldn't have been at the plaza at that time. It might take another day or so to go through the list."

Darryl took another sip of his coffee.

They continued to look over the last six months of search history, but nothing stood out as odd.

"Thanks, Joe. Just give me a call when you find something."

A bit discouraged to not have definite answers from the laptop, Darryl got back to his desk to check his voice messages.

The first message started, "Hi, this is Natalie Anderson. I'm calling to see if you have any leads in the case or if you've found anything new that may help find Audrey. That was all. Sorry to bother you, but it's been days and I'm really scared for her." Natalie choked up at this point then paused to compose herself. "Please call me if there's anything I can do to help."

Darryl wrote a note on his legal pad to call the girl back by the end of the day. He then hit the option to listen to his second message.

"Good morning. This is Lisa Campbell from the adoption agency. I received the court order from your office this morning for the Jennings's file. Everything seems to be in order so I'll have an electronic copy of the file sent to your precinct this afternoon."

There was a pause, then she continued. "Also, since I was the lawyer who proceeded over the Jennings's adoption, I think it'll be beneficial for you to call me back. There was a call to my office a few months ago from someone asking about Audrey's adoption. With Audrey missing, it might mean something. Anyway, I'll be in the office until at least five tonight, which is about six your time. Talk to you soon."

Darryl quickly dialed the lawyer's number.

"Detective, it's good to hear from you. I take it you got my message?"

"Yes, thank you. You said something about a call made to your office earlier this year regarding my missing girl?"

"That's correct. The adoption took place over eighteen years prior to the call, and it was a closed adoption. It was strange, because the call wasn't coming from the biological mother, but from a man. Unfortunately, he didn't give me his name. As you'll see from the file I'm providing, there's no male relative who knows about the adoption. Audrey's mother told us that no one else knew about her child. That's why it stuck out in my mind as odd when I got the call back in early May."

*That timing can't be coincidental.* "Are you sure it was early May?"

"Yes. I checked our phone log after leaving you the voice mail in case you asked. The call came in on May 2nd. Does this date hold any relevance for your case?"

"It could. Do you remember what the man asked specifically?"

"He asked if we had an adoption on file for a child of a Marissa Carter that would've taken place late September to early October of 1998. Since he didn't give his name, and more importantly, it was a closed adoption, I told the gentleman that if we had presided over such an adoption, I couldn't provide him with any details."

"What was the man's response to that?"

"He got angry. Then it was like something dawned on him, and he hung up the phone. I apologize, I forgot to write down the phone number he called from. I'll go through our phone log again and get it. I'll text it to your cell phone."

The detective thanked her for the help before the call ended.

Darryl quickly jotted down the details of their conversation.

There was one thing that stuck out to him. *Who knew that Marissa Carter was pregnant? And even more puzzling, how did they know when she got pregnant? Audrey's birth date was October 2nd, and the man asked about Marissa Carter having a child in late September or early October. If Audrey's father died before she was born, then who knew the intimate details of Marissa's pregnancy?*

Darryl knew exactly who could answer this question; he just had to locate Marissa Carter to ask her.

# Chapter 21

Encouraged by this new development in the case, Darryl was motivated more than ever to find Audrey's biological mother. But he couldn't understand why it was so difficult to locate this woman. *What's she hiding from? Or maybe the more accurate question is—who is she hiding from?*

Darryl hoped there was information in the adoption file that would help his search. *Maybe the deceased father's name will provide information, or maybe Marissa's maiden name. Unless she and the father weren't married, and Carter is her maiden name.*

As he pulled out his legal pad from his desk drawer, the detective saw Audrey's cell phone. *I may as well return it.* And as a bonus, returning the phone gave him an opportunity to see Mel. Darryl deposited the cell phone into its plastic bag and hurried off in the direction of the medical examiner's office.

Entering through the main doors, he was welcomed by the same spunky blonde. "Good morning, detective. Here to see Mel?"

"Yes, I have a piece of evidence to return."

The young woman smiled and picked up her phone. "Detective Harris is here to see you, Ms. Crosby." She winked at Darryl.

*Is the receptionist like this with all the guys?*

Before he could think any more of it, Mel sauntered into the room. "Good morning. What can I do for you?" She gave him a warm smile.

*That smile could brighten anyone's day.* "I'm returning Audrey Jennings's cell phone. I figured you'll need to get it to the evidence room with her other belongings." Darryl smiled back at her as he handed over the cell phone.

"Yes, thanks. Have you come across any new leads in the case?" she asked, while leading him into the kitchen. She found a Styrofoam cup and poured fresh coffee into it, then handed it to Darryl.

*Ah, so she remembers how much I like my coffee.* "I think so. I'm waiting on the adoption file on our missing girl, but I need to contact the biological mother as soon as possible. According to the adoption lawyer, there was a man trying to reach out to the agency about Audrey's adoption. It might be the same guy who resembles Audrey who was staring at her at one of her volleyball matches." He blew on his hot coffee before taking a sip.

"You do have a lot of moving pieces to this case, don't you? The missing girl was put up for adoption. You believe she was pregnant when she was abducted. And there may be someone related to her who was trying to contact her. Do you think this relative could be involved with Audrey's disappearance?" Mel asked as she poured herself a cup of coffee. Her big brown eyes then looked up into his.

"Could be. Or it might just be a coincidence. I assume the biological mother will know who our mystery man is. According to Audrey's adoptive parents, Audrey's father passed away before the adoption process started."

"Do you think the biological mother lied about the father being dead? Do you think that's who's looking for Audrey?" She ushered the detective over to a box of pastries on another counter.

"If the caller was the same man who was seen at the volleyball match, then no. He couldn't have been old enough to be Audrey's biological father. The witness believes the guy to be in his late twenties to early thirties. That would make him no older than sixteen when Audrey was born." Darryl chose an apple fritter from the box Mel was holding open.

She pulled out a Boston crème donut for herself and led Darryl to the small table in the corner. They each took a bite of their pastries.

"Have you considered running Audrey's DNA to see what matches come up in the system? Maybe you can locate this mysterious blood relative that way. Or if you're having difficulties finding the mother, it could help with your search in finding her."

"You're amazing! That's exactly what needs to be done. Can you process Audrey's DNA for me and run it through IAFIS and the other various databases? I know Audrey's parents already provided some of her personal items."

"That shouldn't be a problem. I'll process the items this morning and should have the results for you before you get back from lunch."

"If that's the case, then I owe you lunch. How does food truck food sound?"

"Only if it's from Southern Comfort. They have the best shrimp and grits."

"Shrimp and grits it is. I'll be back by one. Thank you for your help." Darryl popped the last bite of his fritter into his mouth.

"No worries, it's my job. You really don't have to get me lunch."

He gazed into her eyes for a few seconds before she revealed a playful smile.

*I'd do anything for that smile.*

Mel finished her donut and returned to her workspace to run Audrey's DNA. Having left the kitchen at the same time as Mel, Darryl hurried back to the precinct to see if the adoption file had come in.

As he stepped into the main room, he heard, "Detective Harris, can you come to my office?"

*He must be looking for my report.*

"Hey, Captain," Darryl said before taking a seat.

"We received the adoption file on Audrey Jennings. A copy is being printed at the front desk. Once you've gone over it, give me a summary of what you find."

"Of course." Darryl then went on to explain to his boss about his conversation with the adoption lawyer and about his request to have Audrey's DNA ran for possible matches.

Captain Reynolds sat back in his seat as he took in the details.

"And the laptop didn't provide much information for the case. There was an interesting search in Audrey's web history regarding adoption. Unfortunately, though, the timing of the search was around the time she might've known about her pregnancy."

"So, we don't know if she was looking into her own adoption or doing research for her child." Captain Reynolds tapped his index finger against the arm of his chair. "Let me know what the DNA search brings back and make sure I get everything in your report. Preferably by the end of the day."

When his boss went back to reviewing the file he was reading before their discussion, Darryl replied, "You got it."

As he took a seat at his desk, Cathy handed Darryl the adoption file. "Here you go."

"Just what I've been waiting for. Thank you."

When she walked away, Darryl quickly flipped through the thirty plus pages in the file folder.

Then he saw it—or more accurately—he saw the missing information. There was no name listed where the father's name was supposed to be on the legal paperwork.

*How is this possible? How can it be considered a legal adoption if the father's name isn't even on it? Didn't the adoption agency need to verify he passed away by searching for his death certificate? Something isn't right.*

Pulling out his legal pad, he found the lawyer's direct number and gave her a call.

"This is Lisa Campbell. How may I help you?"

"Hi, Lisa. This is Detective Harris. Do you have time to talk about the file you sent over?"

"Yes, I do."

"I've reviewed the documents and noticed the biological father's name isn't listed. I don't see it on any of the paperwork, including the actual adoption form signed by the biological mother and the adoptive parents. How can Audrey's adoption be deemed legal without the father's name?"

After a long exhale, she replied, "I was hoping you'd be able to contact Ms. Carter about this. But since Audrey is missing, it might be best just to tell you." After a deep breath, she continued. "Marissa Carter was raped. That was how she became pregnant with Audrey. She never reported the incident and assured our office she had no idea who the father was."

"Okay . . ." Darryl's voice trailed off.

"Marissa contacted our office when she was already six months pregnant. So trying to convince her to go to the police was useless at that point. She was determined to put the incident behind her and to give Audrey the best home possible."

"Mr. and Mrs. Jennings told me the father had passed away. Whose idea was it to lie to them?"

There was silence on the other end of the line for far too long. Finally, the lawyer answered sheepishly, "It was my boss's idea. Trying to get a child adopted in that situation can be difficult, and Marissa didn't want the rape to be included in the adoption records. I know it was dishonest, but it wasn't my call to make."

"Is there anything else that's missing from this file or that's misleading that I should know about? It could mean life or death for Ms. Jennings."

"No, everything else in the file is accurate. And I'll get the phone number of the mystery caller to you within the hour. I'm sorry for what happened to Audrey. If her disappearance has anything to do with the lie that was told to her adoptive parents, then I don't know how I can make things right."

"I'm working another angle in finding the guy who was looking for Audrey so let's keep our fingers crossed I find him."

After hanging up with Lisa, Darryl remembered the other angle he was talking about—the beautiful CSI who was expecting shrimp and grits in less than an hour. Darryl collected his car keys and hurried out the door hoping he had more luck with the DNA search than with the adoption file.

*If anyone can come through for me, I would bet on Mel providing the next big lead.*

# Chapter 22

She was up before the light came on. It felt like morning, but Audrey had no way of knowing how early it was. She gauged the time of day on two factors: When the light came on in her room, and the temperature outside when she took a shower or was chained to the lawn chair.

The oatmeal left on her plate yesterday attracted more ants than she was used to seeing. They came out in such swarms, that when her kidnapper brought her dinner, he mumbled profanities under his breath as he carried away the bug-ridden plate.

It made Audrey smile inwardly at the irritation it caused him. The dinner he brought her last night was chunks of corned beef, a side of corn, and a buttered roll. Two more bottles of water accompanied the meal. Since there was no midday meal in between what breakfast and dinner must've been, Audrey decided it best to eat it all no matter how it tasted.

Her kidnapper hadn't said a word to her during that visit, but she figured it was for the best. Less conversation meant she couldn't make him angrier than he already had been. However, it was psychologically hard for her not to hear another person's voice at any point during the day.

Waking up this morning, Audrey had immediately tasted the corned beef from last night. The fuzzy film coating her teeth made her desperately want to brush them. Which she only got to do during her shower routine—every other day. If she could keep her kidnapper from getting angry with her for a day or two, maybe she could request to brush her teeth more frequently. It was a challenge, though, seeing as everything set the guy's temper off.

When the lightbulb on the ceiling illuminated the space around her, she started to sit up on the mattress. Audrey automatically adjusted herself as modestly as she could when she heard her kidnapper on the other side of the door.

He stepped around the door and glanced down at the empty plate on the floor. A smug smile spread across the hole his face mask.

Audrey noticed he was wearing jeans and a dark shirt with his work boots. But he no longer wore the black gloves.

"Put your shoes on. We're going outside."

Once the blindfold was on, he led her down the hallway. They stepped outside and made the now familiar few yards to the shower.

*Why the shoes?*

He pulled off her blindfold and pointed to the shower. "Get in. There's another dress for you in there."

Audrey didn't attempt to delay the situation anymore, since it only resulted in a creepy threat.

Now that she was out of the room and in the sunlight, she did her best to ignore the stranger staring at her behind. After washing her hair, lathering up with soap, and rinsing, she dried herself off with the towel.

The dress she pulled off the same ledge was the one she recently wore, with spaghetti straps and considerably shorter than the one she just took off. It hardly passed her thighs. Fortunately, it appeared as though it had been washed since the last time she wore it.

Audrey stepped out of the shower and slipped her shoes back on. With the blindfold back over her eyes, her kidnapper led her on the long walk to the lawn chair, where she was handcuffed.

"Don't move." His footsteps got quieter as he walked away.

It was warm out, but not quite hot. Audrey guessed it must be around eight or nine o'clock in the morning, since the temperature didn't feel higher than in the 80's. The humidity, however, was already soaring, making her uncombed hair frizz as it dried.

She hadn't taken allergy medicine since being kidnapped, and she was suddenly feeling the effects of the pollen in the air. Without warning, she sneezed, not once, but twice in a row.

To her horror, the blindfold fell from her face to rest around her neck. Audrey frantically tried to adjust it back up over her eyes before he noticed, but because the handcuffs were chained down, she couldn't lift her hands. There was nothing she could do.

Daring to look up, she saw her captor about twenty yards straight ahead of her feeding hay to two large horses—a white stallion and a painted horse with brown and white spots. Her kidnapper was inside the corral with the horses and hadn't yet noticed that she was watching him.

After he cleaned the horses' hooves with some kind of hook contraption, he pulled out a large brush from a tote bag next to him on the ground. Starting with the mane, he brushed each horse. He moved on to stroking the back of the white stallion as he talked softly to the animal, then rubbed the other horse's face.

The love and tenderness he showed these animals was out of character from how he treated Audrey. She felt an unexpected wave of jealousy. *Why is he such a monster to me but so caring to his horses?*

Forcing herself to ignore those feelings, it suddenly hit her: *He isn't wearing his mask! Oh my god!*

The realization came mere seconds before he turned in her direction and saw her staring at him. The hostility in his expression made her want to crawl into a hole and die.

He dropped the brush and ducked under the fence to march toward her.

She was a sitting duck. *What's he going to do to me? He won't believe it was an accident!*

He crossed the distance between them in record time, and as he stood in front of her, he pulled back his arm and slapped her across the face. She instantly heard high-pitched ringing in her left ear.

Her left cheek was stinging so badly she wanted to cry. Before he could hit her again, she bent her upper half to block her stomach as much as she could. There was no way of knowing what his fury would lead him to do next.

He was still raging but didn't hit her again. Instead, he said through clenched jaw, "You know this means I can't let you leave here alive?"

Audrey cautiously sat back up in the chair to look into his eyes. A tear rolled down her cheek as she whispered, "Wasn't that the plan all along?"

"I guess you'll never know." He uncuffed her from the chair and snatched her arm, squeezing it hard enough that a cry escaped her lips.

Even though he was only a few inches taller than her, his quick stride made it hard for her to keep up with his pace. The fact that she was wearing flip flops didn't help the situation. She tripped on an uneven patch of ground and fell.

The grip he had on her arm didn't give so she was dragged a few yards along the way.

*What's he going to do to me? Is he thinking about the baby?* Thoughts continued to race through her mind.

They were within arm's reach of the door when he realized Audrey didn't have her blindfold on. He stopped and shoved it over her eyes.

When they got into the room, without warning, he threw her onto the mattress.

The force of her body hitting the mattress made the blindfold fall around her neck again. She looked up at him with eyes full of unshed tears. There was no way for her to know what was going through his head, but she knew it wasn't good.

Another few seconds crept by before he retreated from the room, slamming the door behind him.

Audrey was petrified he'd return to torture or kill her for something she hadn't done on purpose. Her heart racing, she began to pray that her kidnapper wouldn't end her life.

Nothing happened for a few minutes, then a half hour passed. Afraid to move in case he came back any moment, Audrey went over the stranger's features in her mind. He had dark hair and a five o'clock shadow. There was something oddly familiar about him. *Where have I seen him before?*

Then the memory raced back to her! He had been staring at her when she was alone at the mall over a week ago. She hadn't thought much about it at the time. But now she wondered if he was there because of her, or was that the first time he had seen her?

# Chapter 23

By one o'clock in the afternoon, Darryl had returned to the medical examiner's office with his and Mel's lunches. The receptionist recognized him right away and got on the phone to call Mel. The blonde gave him another one of her winks.

Unsure of her intentions, he just gave her a small smile and ambled over to the bench to wait for Mel. Less than a minute later, she came around the corner carrying a manila folder under her left arm. "Hi, there. Come on back. I have some good news for you," she said with a big grin on her face.

Darryl followed her to the kitchen where he started unloading their Styrofoam boxes of food. "Here you go. Shrimp and grits and a bottled water."

"Thanks," Mel replied as she took the items from him.

"So, you were saying something about good news." He opened his Styrofoam container to reveal a turkey club sandwich on whole wheat with a side of seasoned French fries.

"Audrey's DNA came back with not one, but two matches. The first is a maternal match, which is from her biological mother." She flipped open the manila folder to show Darryl the search results.

"The search came from an employer-provided DNA sample. Looks like your missing girl's mother, Marissa Kennedy, works at a nursing home in Jacksonville, Florida. Or at least she did two years ago when her DNA was registered. It's common for those types of care facilities to require employees' DNA when they work with vulnerable patients."

*Marissa Kennedy—no wonder I couldn't locate her. She changed her name. But why didn't I find a marriage license for her in my search?*

He pulled out the sheet with the results and took a generous bite out of his sandwich as he read it.

Mel removed the cover from the plastic container in her box. Using the plastic spoon that was also in the box, she scooped up a large shrimp with some cheesy grits and took a bite. "Mm, creamy and spicy."

He smiled at the delight that was evident on her face. Glancing back at the document in his hand, he said, "This is great, Mel. I should be able to locate Marissa through the employer who registered her DNA." Darryl beamed as he looked at her. If he didn't know better, he could swear she was blushing from his remark. "You said there were two matches?"

"Yes, the second is a sibling match. More accurately, a half-sibling match. However, this half-sibling's DNA doesn't match Marissa's DNA. This confirms Audrey's biological father has a son." She handed Darryl a second sheet of DNA results.

"Audrey has a half-brother from her father's side? Do we know who this half-brother is?"

"Yes, his DNA is in the system due to the young man being suspected of rape approximately ten years ago. His name is Aaron Smith, and he was a junior at the University of Chicago at the time the allegations were made. The case never went to court, because it was settled between the parties before it made it to trial. However, Aaron's DNA had already been processed," Mel finished, then took another bite of her grits.

"Wow, what a guy," Darryl said sarcastically.

"There's something else you should know in case you plan to question the half-brother," Mel said as Darryl read the second document. "He's the son of a well-known lawyer in Chicago. That may be why he got off on the rape charges—if he was guilty anyway. Just be careful how you go about questioning him."

"Good call. I'll make sure I'm by the book with him." He gave her an appreciative grin and was rewarded with a smile in return.

As they finished their lunches, Darryl said, "I owe you dinner for all the information you gathered for me."

"Let me know when and where," Mel said enticingly over her shoulder as they parted ways.

Minutes later, Darryl dropped the manila folder onto his desk. *Finally, some real leads.* Not quite sure how he was going to go about questioning Aaron, he decided to reach out to Audrey's biological mother first. Getting the name of the nursing home she worked at from the information Mel provided him, Darryl pulled up the Elderly Care with Heart nursing home online and made the call.

"Good afternoon. Elderly Care with Heart. Jill speaking. How may I help you?"

"Hi. I'm looking for Marissa Carter, sorry, I mean Marissa Kennedy. Is she working today?"

"Yes, I believe she's with a patient. Let me put you on hold for a moment. May I ask who's calling?"

"I'm a detective from Cocoa Beach calling regarding a missing girl."

After letting out a gasp, Jill replied, "Oh my goodness, let me get her for you right away."

A minute later the other end of the line was picked back up. "This is Marissa."

"Good afternoon, Marissa. This is Detective Harris. I'm working a missing person's case in Cocoa Beach. I believe you know the victim, Audrey Jennings. I have evidence she's your biological daughter."

With a catch in her voice, she asked just above a whisper, "Audrey is missing? How long has she been gone?"

"She was reported missing last Friday—four days ago. Her adoptive parents are extremely worried about her. They only revealed the fact that Audrey was adopted when a development in the case made it necessary."

"What development?" Marissa asked, bewildered, and obviously trying to hold her emotions together.

"A witness saw a young man in his late twenties to early thirties at one of Audrey's volleyball matches a few months back. He said the young man was a male look-alike of Audrey."

"No, it can't be."

"Does that mean you know who this mystery man is?"

"I don't know how he could've found out about Audrey."

"How *who* could've found out about her?"

"Aaron Smith, the son of the man who raped me. He was only twelve when it happened, and I left the house and never returned. I didn't tell anyone who Audrey's father was."

"How did you know Aaron and his father?"

Marissa began to cry. "I was Aaron's nanny. He was always getting into trouble at school and was a handful for his father, who was a widower. I worked for Jeremy Smith taking care of Aaron since he was nine years old. His father began acting a little too friendly toward me a few years into my employment there. I should've left that job before he had the chance to take advantage of me."

"What happened to you was not your fault. You were just a young woman doing your job." After giving her time to compose herself, Darryl continued. "Do you think it's possible Aaron has something to do with Audrey's disappearance?"

Marissa's confident reply promptly followed. "Yes. He was an awful child with a lot of problems. There's no telling how he turned out or what delusions he has about Audrey if he knows about her existence. The last I heard from my family that lives in Chicago, Jeremy Smith passed away last year. He left everything to Aaron, even after the whole ordeal with the rape charge against him when he was in college."

*So, she heard about that.*

"Marissa, I've had a difficult time locating you. Your last name has changed, but I never came across any records in my search to indicate you had gotten married. How is it that you're now Marissa Kennedy?"

"After Audrey was born, I started using my mother's maiden name, Kennedy. This way Jeremy Smith couldn't find me."

"If you don't mind me asking, why didn't you press charges against Jeremy Smith for what he did to you?"

"After he raped me, he told me he was one of the best lawyers in the area, and that no one would believe me if I went to the police."

*That sneaky bastard.* "I'm very sorry for what you went through."

"Detective, please find Audrey. I may not have been able to raise her, but I've loved her from the moment I found out I was pregnant, despite what happened. Don't let the Smith family get away with hurting anyone else." Marissa started getting choked up again.

"I'll do everything I can to find her."

After providing his work and cell phone numbers and gaining Marissa's personal number, Darryl ended the call.

The disgust he felt toward the deceased Jeremy Smith and his delinquent son was causing fury to build in him. Unfortunately, while there was nothing Darryl could do about Jeremy Smith, it was time to see what Aaron had to say about his half-sister's disappearance.

# Chapter 24

After hanging up with Marissa, Darryl noticed he had a text message from Lisa Campbell. It was the phone number of the mystery caller who asked about Audrey's adoption.

He dialed the number on his work phone and anxiously waited for an answer. Then came the frustrating automated message: "The number you have dialed is not in service."

*That figures.* He typed the phone number into the database he pulled up on his screen. The result came up showing the number as registered to a burner phone. *Another dead end.* Taking out the search results from the manila folder Mel gave him earlier, Darryl scanned the document for information that could help him find Aaron.

Just then his work phone rang. "This is Detective Harris."

"Hi Darryl, it's Joe. I have an update on the van we saw on the thrift store security video."

"That's great! Go ahead."

"I was able to zoom in on the van's dashboard. There's a parking permit sitting in the corner, on the side by the driver's door. The permit is for the Elks Lodge in Cape Canaveral, which is only a few miles away. They wouldn't verify anything over the phone when I called them earlier so I stopped by the lodge after lunch to talk with the gentleman who organizes their events."

"So, were you able to get the name of the owner of the van?"

"Sorry to give you bad news, but the van was stolen. The owner passed away a month ago, and his widow reported it stolen the day Audrey went missing. I couldn't get any hits on the ball-capped man either. There wasn't enough of his face on the security footage to identify him."

"I appreciate your help with reviewing the footage. Looks like I'm down to my last lead at this point."

"Good luck. I hope you catch the guy."

Now even more determined to get in contact with his next possible suspect, Darryl searched online for an Aaron Smith in the Chicago area. Calculating his age based on the fact that Marissa said Aaron was twelve when she got pregnant with Audrey, he figured Aaron was approximately thirty or thirty-one.

Waiting for his search results to populate, Darryl walked to the kitchen for a cup of coffee and a snack. Pulling his wallet from his back pocket, he took out a dollar bill and stuck it into the only vending machine the station had. Being one of the few healthier options, Darryl chose a bag of pretzels.

With his coffee in one hand and pretzels in the other, he got back to his desk to see if his search was successful.

But to his dismay, he sat down to see a list of twenty-nine Aaron Smiths fitting the description.

While contemplating the fastest way of narrowing down this list, something came back to him. *Marissa mentioned Aaron inherited all of his father's possessions when he died. It's possible Aaron lives in the home he was raised in. The same home Marissa was attacked in.*

Searching for the personal information of Aaron's father, Jeremy Smith, Darryl was able to find the address of the house at 100 Malcolm Court in Chicago. Another quick property-appraisal search confirmed it was now owned by Aaron. Typing the address into a public records search, Darryl located a phone number and dialed it.

"Good afternoon. The Smith residence," a young woman answered.

"Hi, this is Detective Harris of the Cocoa Beach Police. I need to speak with Aaron Smith. It's regarding a time-sensitive matter."

"Mr. Smith is at the office. Can I get your name and number so he can call you back when he gets home?" she replied as if his comment about it being a "time-sensitive matter" wasn't a factor.

"Actually, can you give me his cell phone number? I need to reach him right away."

"I'm not at liberty to give out that information, but if you want me to call him and give him the information when we get off the phone, I can do that. I can't promise you'll get a call back right away though. Mr. Smith is very busy."

Sensing he was getting nowhere fast with this woman, Darryl gave her his cell phone number and reiterated the urgency of the matter.

Once the call had ended, he started to feel defeat sink in.

Tearing open his bag of pretzels, he thought back on his original theories regarding this case.

Darryl now determined that if Aaron was the man responsible for Audrey's disappearance, then he was confident this case wasn't related to the Cocoa Beach Killer. The profile of his serial killer was of someone who would now be in their early to late forties, making Aaron much too young to be the same guy.

That didn't mean Audrey wasn't in danger or that she was even alive at this point. It did mean, however, that Darryl needed to find Aaron's motive in wanting his sister kidnapped.

Audrey had a closed adoption. Even her biological mother hadn't tried reaching out to her. *What's he trying to gain by having Audrey disappear?* Then a possibility came to mind. *Maybe it isn't what he intends to GAIN but what he wants to KEEP that resulted in his decision to have her go missing.*

Darryl returned his attention to his computer and searched for "Jeremy Smith: Last Will and Testament."

According to his previous search, Mr. Smith died back in January. *His will could be public record by now.* Combing through a list of legal documents, Darryl located Mr. Smith's will and started to read through the fifty-six-page document. When he got to the beneficiary section of the legal form, he found the smoking gun.

The wording in this section specifically stated that all assets of Jeremy Smith's estate would be divided proportionately to all living descendants of the deceased. *It's possible Aaron didn't want to share his inheritance with his half-sibling. But this doesn't explain how Aaron found out about Audrey's existence.* Darryl would need to get Aaron to divulge this information.

Since he wasn't going to hold his breath that he'd get a call back from his newest suspect any time soon, Darryl grabbed his car keys and legal pad and left the precinct to get fresh air. He'd need to think through his line of questions. His instincts told him Mel was right—this guy was going to be a hard one to crack.

When he returned to the precinct two hours later with his list of questions in hand, Darryl confidently settled into his chair. While waiting on a call from Aaron, he planned on digging deeper into the young man's past.

Something had been bothering Darryl since he spoke with Marissa earlier that day. She mentioned Aaron had started getting into trouble at an early age. *Why was that?*

*Was it the result of his upbringing or being a blood relative of Jeremy Smith?*

He was delving through records on Aaron and his father when his work phone rang. "This is Detective Harris."

"Hi. This is Margaret Jennings. I'm calling to see if you've heard anything about Audrey. I know we spoke yesterday, but Daniel and I are very worried."

"I'm sorry, Mrs. Jennings. We've been following a few different leads. I have a message from Natalie from this morning as well. I don't have anything definite yet to tell you all, but as soon as I do, I'll make sure to pass on the information."

"Okay, I'll call Natalie and let her know. She and Keith have been keeping in touch with us. They want to help in any way they can to get Audrey back home."

"I appreciate the help you all have provided. If anything comes up, I'll let you know."

When they said their good-byes and ended the call, Darryl resumed his search of the Smith men's pasts. A legal document suddenly aroused his interest: The divorce papers of a Jeremy Smith and Catherine Smith.

*Divorce? That can't be right. Didn't Marissa say Jeremy was a widower? Maybe Catherine was a first or second wife and not Aaron's mother.* It only took a few minutes to pull up Aaron's birth certificate online. *There it is. His mother is Catherine Smith. So, it was a lie.*

*Aaron's mother didn't die—or at least that wasn't the reason for Jeremy Smith's single status years ago.*

Darryl suspected that if Jeremy Smith wanted people to believe his wife had died, there must've been a reason for the falsehood. Going back further in his search, he came across multiple police reports where Catherine Smith reported that Jeremy Smith had physically abused her. However, none of the accusations resulted in jail time.

*He must've been able to manipulate his way out of those situations like he did with Marissa.* But the thing that confused the detective the most was the fact that the divorce papers gave full custody of Aaron to his father. *How much influence did this guy have in Chicago?*

While reviewing other search results, Darryl got another phone call, but this time on his cell phone.

"This is Detective Harris."

"Yes, I believe you've been looking for me," a male voice replied. "This is Aaron Smith. You called my residence earlier and spoke with my housekeeper."

Darryl pulled out his pad of paper and pen. "Aaron, thank you for your time."

"You mentioned it was regarding a time-sensitive matter. How can I help you?" Aaron responded impatiently.

Darryl didn't like the vibe he was getting from this guy. "You're correct. I'm calling from Cocoa Beach, Florida, about a missing girl. She disappeared last Friday, and none of her family or friends seem to know where she is."

"A missing girl. Wow. But what does that have to do with me?"

"The missing girl is your half-sister, Audrey. I believe you were recently in Florida to see her, at a high school volleyball match back in May."

Taking his time, Aaron finally replied, "Actually I was in Florida for business. Even though I was able to make it to her game, I didn't have time to talk to Audrey afterwards."

"How'd you find out about your half-sister? Her mother and adoptive parents had agreed upon a closed adoption."

Another long pause on the other end of the line. "It was unfortunate for me to be hiding in the closet of the room where my father and his mistress, Marissa, were having relations."

Darryl was taken aback by Aaron's misconception of what went down between his father and Marissa. "How did you know their 'relations' resulted in a pregnancy? I spoke with Audrey's biological mother recently, and she made it sound like no one was aware except her and those involved in the adoption proceedings."

"I wouldn't believe anything Marissa has to say. She's just the whore my father hired to babysit me," came Aaron's venomous response.

*Good, he's starting to unravel.* "That doesn't answer my question. How'd you know about Audrey?"

"I didn't know for sure Marissa got knocked up until my father died. At that point, I had a private investigator look into the matter."

Darryl digested this information. "Okay, but how were you able to locate her, given her adoption was closed?"

He heard the heavy breathing of his agitated caller and awaited what was coming next.

"I figured now that my half-sibling was an adult, she deserved to know the truth about her real family. And regarding how I found her—well, money talks."

Fully aware he wasn't getting truthful answers to his line of questioning, Darryl moved on. "Why didn't you stay after the volleyball match to introduce yourself?"

"I told you I was in Florida on business. I had a meeting early the next morning in Chicago, and the volleyball game went long. I figured I'd get back to Florida when the opportunity surfaced again."

*Unbelievable. He has an answer for everything. But none of it sounds like the truth.*

"Why don't you give me the exact time Audrey went missing. If I have an alibi for the time she disappeared, then you can stop the questions and move on to someone else as a suspect."

The guy's patronizing tone was starting to get under Darryl's skin. "Audrey was last seen at around one o'clock in the afternoon last Friday."

Without skipping a beat, Aaron replied, "Well then, there it is. I was in a business meeting with ten other associates at that time, here in my office in Chicago. I'll send you a list of my colleagues that were in attendance."

"Yes, please do. I'll need to verify their stories and get back to you with any more questions. Can I have your direct number? Maybe a cell phone number?"

"That's okay. You can call the house and leave a message with my housekeeper if you need me," he replied smugly.

Struggling to keep his professional composure, Darryl managed to thank Aaron for his time before he hung up. *This is my guy. Aaron Smith is an egotistical bastard who thinks he's untouchable, just like his father.*

Little did Aaron know, Darryl wasn't going to let him get away with whatever he did or was planning to do to Audrey.

# Chapter 25

Audrey engraved another small line into the wall behind her pillow. She had broken off all but one of her fingernails by keeping up with her makeshift calendar. But time was nonexistent if she didn't continue this routine.

Today there was a total of forty-seven lines, making it October second, her nineteenth birthday. It had been over six weeks since her blindfold slipped from her eyes, and she reaped the punishment of that unfortunate incident. Her captor hadn't hit her since, but he barely stopped himself on multiple occasions when he had gotten angry with her.

He continued to turn the light on each day for a good part of the day and took her out most days for time in the lawn chair. The only difference was now she only wore a mask to move from her room to the outside. Her showers occurred every other day on average, and she got two meals a day. Her kidnapper rarely spoke to her and normally glared at her if she tried to start conversations.

Audrey was beyond lonely stuck in this jail-like room. The only thing keeping her sane was the child growing within her. Now that she was fourteen weeks along, her abdomen was expanding. While she no longer included sit-ups in her exercise routine, she continued with the rest of her workout.

Having limited things to keep her busy each day, it became habit for Audrey to leave at least a few morsels of food behind at each meal to entice her ant buddies out for a visit. Between being pregnant and a lack of entertainment, sleeping over twelve hours a day had become another part of her routine.

When she was halfway done with her exercises, she stopped to drink some water. As she guzzled the last swig of the bottle, the locks on the door started to turn. She quickly sat back down on the mattress so the stranger wouldn't become suspicious of her activities.

Audrey had been extremely troubled recently, wondering why her kidnapper was at the mall the day she saw him. But she didn't dare bring it up. Who knew what he'd do if she asked. She shivered at the thought.

He came in wearing his scrubs and work boots, but he no longer saw the need for the ski mask. The plate of food he was holding included a sandwich on whole wheat, a red apple, and a bag of potato chips. He set two more bottles of water near the plate on the floor.

The ants had finished off the crumbs from last night's meal while Audrey slept so nothing was left. Her kidnapper snatched the plate and turned to leave.

"Today's my birthday," she said while keeping her focus on her lap. The comment surprised her as much as it did him. Sensing no movement in the direction of the door, she glanced over at the stranger and saw he was staring at her with a blank expression on his face.

Without saying a word, he shut the door behind him.

It didn't come as a surprise since he treated her like the scum of the Earth. She hadn't shed any more tears, not since being slapped in the face. *There's no point in crying anymore.*

Audrey got up to quickly finish her exercises, not wanting to share her whole meal with her tiny roommates. When she finished her exercise routine, she picked up the plate and one of her bottled waters.

Her prenatal vitamin was included with this meal. The sandwich was made up of egg salad with a slice of cheddar cheese. Strange combination, but she couldn't afford to dismiss any of her meals. Ever since the incident with her blindfold, her meals have been less reliable. Most days she got two meals and a couple of bottles of water at each meal, but there were days when she only got one meal and a random snack with her water.

Audrey ate a majority of the sandwich but left a piece of crust behind for the ants to haul away later. She picked up the red apple and took a bite of the juicy fruit. The chips she'd save for later—in case her kidnapper didn't bring her any more food the rest of the day.

Audrey lay back down on the mattress and recalled the day she found out she was pregnant.

***

It had been late July. She had gotten back from her shift at the Mirage Resort. After taking a shower, she had reached under her bathroom sink for her hair dryer and saw her feminine products. It occurred to her she should need them soon. Pulling up her calendar on her cell phone, she saw the reminder she had setup last month. It was for three days ago.

Feeling a wave of panic, but not wanting to overreact, Audrey threw on her clothes and headed to her room. She put on her shoes and collected her car keys and purse. Before running out of the house, she told her parents she was meeting up with Natalie for dinner.

It had taken her a few minutes to figure out a place she could get a pregnancy test without the risk of running into someone she knew. Since she'd bought herself time with her lie about meeting Natalie, Audrey had driven about fifteen miles north to the next town.

She purchased a pregnancy test from the first pharmacy she came across and used the store's restroom to take the test. The positive reading came up within seconds of her following the instructions on the box.

***

*That was over two months ago.* Audrey gazed at the ceiling and wondered what her family and friends were doing today. *Are they worried sick about me? Is today especially hard for them since it's my birthday and they don't know if I'm dead or alive?* Her heart hurt for what they must be going through. Turning to her side, she tried to fall asleep and let the day pass as quickly as possible.

Many hours later, the locks began to turn again.

He marched in carrying her blindfold. When it was over her eyes, he led her out of the building. She guessed it was late afternoon by this point. The sun was less intense, and the temperature was around seventy-five degrees. Since the blindfold had been removed when they got outside, Audrey could see fluffy white clouds dispersed across the light blue sky.

She had always loved the fall weather in Florida. The humidity decreased along with the temperature, but it was still warm enough to enjoy going to the pool or surfing in the ocean.

When they got to the lawn chair, he handcuffed her and left her to tend to his horses.

Audrey sat and watched the sun as it set. Brilliant hues of orange and purple spread across the vast sky. She was thankful for the beauty in front of her. It was as if God Himself gifted it to her for her birthday. Trying to hide the smile this brought to her face, she looked down at her lap. The last thing she wanted was to upset her captor and get hit on her birthday.

When he finished feeding and grooming his horses, her kidnapper came back to uncuff her and lead her away. With her blindfold back in place, they quietly strode through the hallway and on to her secluded room.

After he left, Audrey struggled to keep her emotions at bay. *Will I have to spend another birthday in this room?*

Twenty minutes had passed before he returned, carrying in a plate of food. While it had a few things on it, the one thing that stood out was a cupcake with white frosting. Then Audrey noticed he was carrying a book and a small brush in the crook of his other arm.

He placed everything on the floor.

Audrey looked at the items curiously.

"The brush better not have a bristle missing when I inspect it each day, or I'll beat you with it. I could care less if you read the book or not. And don't get any ideas—none of it was my idea." He then took the empty plate from earlier that day and locked the door behind him.

Audrey stared at the items for a moment before carefully getting up from the mattress and shuffling over to inspect them. Her hair hadn't been brushed since the morning she was kidnapped. Her captor only allowed her a minute to comb through her thick hair before he took it away from her again. So she had plenty of tangles and knots.

She sat on the floor and poured some water on the bottom half of her hair, knowing the brush would glide through the strands much easier if it was wet.

When she was able to brush through her hair without tangles catching in the bristles, Audrey picked up the book. It was one she had read back in middle school—*Little Women.* It was not only a classic, but it happened to be one of Audrey's favorite books of all time. She smiled to herself. *He'd hate the fact that I love this book.*

Dinner included a plain cheeseburger on a bun, a side of sweet potato fries, and corn. But Audrey chose to eat the cupcake before anything else. *Why not? It's my birthday.* She carefully peeled away the paper wrapper so as not to waste any of the precious treat. There was no way of knowing if she'd get another sweet while she was held captive.

The first bite was heavenly. It was a red velvet cupcake with cream cheese frosting. She savored every moist bite.

Leaving only a piece of the burger's bun for the ants, Audrey took her time eating the cheeseburger, fries, and corn. With a bottle of water in one hand and the book in her other, Audrey got comfortable on the mattress.

As she opened the book to page one, she replayed what her kidnapper said before he left: "None of it was my idea." *Was he lying? And if not, then who else knows I'm being kept here against my will?*

# Chapter 26

It had been six weeks since Darryl first spoke with Aaron Smith about his missing half-sister. While the conversation proved to Darryl that the young man had something to hide, his alibi checked out. Aaron not only had ten other colleagues vouch for his presence at a meeting in Chicago at the time of Audrey's disappearance, but they'd been on a conference call with five other people who also supported Aaron's alibi.

There was still something about Aaron that rubbed Darryl the wrong way. And if he was involved in Audrey's disappearance, then Darryl planned to figure out Aaron's role in her kidnapping.

Darryl had gotten a call from Mr. and Mrs. Jennings every other day, asking about leads. It had been difficult for him to meet with them weeks earlier and explain he had hit a wall with every lead he had. Mrs. Jennings wept right there in the interview room, while Mr. Jennings held her in his arms with his head hung in defeat.

When it came time to tell Keith and Natalie about where he was with Audrey's case, it didn't go any better. It had been crushing to watch a young man sob over the fact that he may have lost his future wife.

Natalie had first wept but then got angry Darryl hadn't done more to find her best friend. She told him she could've done a better job with the case. But he hadn't taken it to heart.

Sitting at his desk early one Monday morning, Darryl drank his coffee while looking over the details of Audrey's case file. He started at the beginning—the Friday she disappeared.

A prior search of Aaron's bank records and credit card statements hadn't resulted in the red flags Darryl had hoped for. There didn't look to be any large payouts to anyone to kidnap Audrey, or any charges to a storage unit or random location where she was being held.

Darryl didn't want to believe the young lady was dead, but now that he no longer believed his serial killer was involved, she just might be. At least the Cocoa Beach Killer held his victims for months before killing them, even if he tortured them during that time.

*Aaron doesn't have a reason to keep her alive.*

Darryl had been beating himself up for the last six weeks. *How can I let another case go cold? Especially when I'm so close to the person I feel is responsible.*

When he tried to locate Aaron's mother, Catherine Smith, the search was harder than he expected. She had remarried a few years after her and Jeremy's divorce and moved to San Diego. When Darryl finally got her on the phone, their conversation didn't result in any useful information.

Catherine had explained how she endured years of physical abuse at the hands of Aaron's father. She had admitted that she hadn't fought for custody of Aaron, because Jeremy would have destroyed her character in court with outright lies. She also hesitantly revealed that at the tender age of eight, Aaron had already been demonstrating the same negative traits as his father by being verbally abusive to her.

In regards to Darryl's prior suspect, Carl Bennett had recently been dismissed as a suspect in the case. His lack of an alibi hadn't been enough to continue the shadow that Captain Reynolds had ordered. In the weeks he'd been shadowed, Carl's limited routine included him driving to and from work with a quick stop at the grocery store once or twice a week.

Darryl had to admit, though, that it had been beneficial to have Carl as a suspect, even for a short time. His interrogation led to the discovery of Aaron Smith, his new prime suspect.

The only positive thing to come out of the last six weeks was Darryl's progressing relationship with Mel.

They had gone on a few dinner dates in the last month in addition to their weekly lunch date at their favorite food truck by the beach.

Their dates consisted of Mel listening intently to Darryl's frustrations with the Jennings's case, while Darryl had been intrigued with Mel's vivid description of evidence she had processed.

Darryl had decided to follow Mel's lead in whatever direction their relationship went. He was just happy to have a second chance with her.

Darryl took a break from reading the case file to get a fresh cup of coffee. As he moseyed into the kitchen, his eyes swept the counters for anything good to eat for breakfast. A loaf of banana-nut bread was sitting on the counter with an end piece already sliced off. After pouring a mug of coffee, he cut off a thick slice of the bread.

Making a mental note to spend an extra ten minutes at the gym that night for eating such a treat, Darryl returned to his desk.

"Harris, can you stop by my office?"

*Ah, Captain Reynolds is in.* Darryl dropped his banana bread off at his desk and headed to his boss's office.

"Good morning, Captain." He took his usual seat.

"Where are we at with the Jennings's case? I have other cases to send your way if you don't have any leads with the missing girl."

Uncomfortable with the idea of letting this case go cold without further investigation, Darryl replied, "I'm taking another look over the file and running some searches on various possible leads."

Captain Reynolds raised a brow. "I'll give you until the end of day tomorrow to find something new that's considered a good lead. If you can't, then I'm putting you on another case."

"I understand. I appreciate the additional time."

At his desk, Darryl slumped into his chair. *What am I missing?*

As he finished reading through the notes he took of Mr. and Mrs. Jennings's interview the day Audrey went missing, the phone rang. "This is Detective Harris."

"Hi, Detective Harris. I was thinking today might be a good day to stop by the food truck. Do you have lunch plans yet?"

He smiled at Mel's use of his title when she normally referred to him by his first name. *She knows how to keep my spirits up, even at a critical time like this.* "I think the food truck is a great idea. How about I swing by around twelve thirty and pick you up?"

Mel gladly accepted his offer.

As Darryl hung up the phone, he saw Mr. Jennings traipsing into the main room of the precinct. Darryl stood and said, "Mr. Jennings, may I help you?"

"I know we spoke yesterday on the phone, but I can't just sit at home when my daughter is missing."

After leading the older gentleman to an interview room, Darryl allowed Mr. Jennings to choose a seat. The detective sat across from him and tried to think of something he could say to comfort the disturbed father.

"I assure you, Mr. Jennings, we're actively investigating your daughter's case. Of course, if you remember anything that occurred around the time Audrey went missing that could be helpful, then you're always welcome to call or come into the station."

"I've gone over and over in my mind the days prior to Audrey's disappearance, and the only thing that sticks out to me is the fact that she was sick for days. The morning she went missing she was making toast, which she normally didn't eat for breakfast." Mr. Jennings rubbed the back of his neck. "My gut was telling me she was pregnant, but I didn't have the heart to ask her."

Doing his best to hide the fact that he already knew this, Darryl replied, "If that was the case, it must've been hard for you not to say anything to her about it."

"Maybe if I had talked to her then things wouldn't have happened as they did. She could be home safe with her family and friends. With everything that has happened, being a grandfather so soon doesn't sound that bad."

Darryl nodded.

"Keith may not have much for ambitions, outside of playing baseball in college and owning his parent's furniture store someday, but it's clear he loves my daughter. And while his parents are overly strict—in my opinion—they've raised a great kid. Keith and Audrey will make wonderful parents, even at such a young age." The sentiment of his statement became too much for Mr. Jennings. He began to sob, his hands quickly covering his face.

Darryl got up and pulled out a couple of tissues from the box nearby before dropping into the seat next to the weeping man. "I'm sorry for what you're going through." He handed over the tissues. "From what I've heard about your daughter, she's a fighter. If anyone has a shot at coming home, she does."

Mr. Jennings grinned momentarily through the tears. "She really does accomplish everything she sets her mind to. I've always admired Audrey for her perseverance."

When Mr. Jennings had had a good cry and had taken time to compose himself, the two men left the interview room and walked toward the main entrance.

"Please don't give up on my daughter, detective. I know how new cases can come up and cases like my daughter's get moved to the bottom of the pile."

"Mr. Jennings, I don't intend to give up on your daughter. She's my number one priority."

Guilt shot through his conscience. *But I can't promise that'll be true as of tomorrow.*

# Chapter 27

The baby moved more often and with greater strength each day. It was the only joy Audrey experienced in this awful place. As if things weren't bad enough, her captor rarely acknowledged her existence except when he had to—such as to turn the light on each morning or take her outside.

Thanksgiving was a month ago, but she wouldn't have known it if it weren't for her improvised calendar hidden behind her pillow. There wasn't any turkey or stuffing or pumpkin pie brought to her that day.

Audrey had refused to let him see the exceptional loneliness she felt. Thanksgiving had always been her father's favorite holiday, and the thought of him sitting at home miserable made her cry, not once, but multiple times that day.

She had thought a lot about her parents since being kidnapped, and about how much they meant to her. *I miss you both dearly.*

Today was Christmas. Audrey placed her hand on her expanding belly and thanked God for the child that was growing within her. Now six months along, her only pregnancy symptoms were heartburn when she ate anything spicy or fried and the need to urinate every hour on the hour. Her baby seemed to have taken up residence on her bladder. *It's worth it though.*

The closer she got to her due date, the tougher it got for her to control the fear that tried to overwhelm her. Knowing there was another person involved in her kidnapping made coming up with an escape plan substantially harder.

*Even if I can get away from the man I've seen for the last few months, can I get past a second kidnapper? And why haven't I seen the other person?*

So many questions and no answers. Now that the light was on, she assumed it was morning. Sitting upright on the mattress, Audrey took care of her daily mark in the wall. Satisfied with the indent, she picked up the bottle of water she left next to the mattress and took a long swig.

After utilizing her crude toilet, which got more difficult to use as her pregnancy progressed, Audrey took out her brush and worked it through her long, thick hair. She opened *Little Women* and began reading the one chapter she allowed herself to read each morning. In the afternoon she'd read the next chapter.

As she got past the second page, she heard the locks begin to turn. Her kidnapper walked in wearing jeans and a black shirt with the blindfold clutched in his right hand. "Get up. We're going outside."

Audrey stood and waited for the blindfold to be placed over her eyes before being led out of the room.

The air outside was cooler today. Cooler than it had been the last few days that she had been out. She guessed it was around fifty degrees. Wearing only the summer dress that was left for her in the shower, she began to shiver.

Her captor hauled her over to the concrete shower and yanked off her blindfold. "Get in."

Audrey did as he said. After turning the shower on, she slowly peeled off the dress, needing its warmth for as long as possible. Once her hair was wet, she reached over to collect her toothbrush and toothpaste.

The shock of the cold hit her like a punch to the gut, and she immediately jumped back under the water to get warm again. *What will happen when the temperature drops even more? I can catch a cold or even pneumonia.* Audrey didn't think he would care unless it affected her unborn child.

When she was done brushing her teeth, she picked up the shampoo bottle and lathered her hair while the rest of her body stayed under the water. Modesty was no longer a concern to her so she ignored the fact that she was exposed to her kidnapper. Blocking him out of her mind had become a coping mechanism to get her through this process.

After she finished showering, Audrey took the faded blue towel off the ledge and simultaneously turned the water off. Drying off as fast as she possibly could, she looked over to see a pair of gray sweatpants and a black long-sleeved shirt for her to wear. *Thank goodness.*

She put the sweatpants on while keeping the towel wrapped around her chest. They were a bit big on her, but they had a drawstring. She adjusted the pants, then slipped the shirt on.

Like clockwork, her captor was at the shower with the blindfold. Seconds later, he led her back into the building and to her lonely room. He whipped the blindfold off her face and turned to pick up her empty plate from the night before.

"I'm having a hard time using that bucket now that I'm getting bigger."

Not expecting a response, she jumped when he replied. "That sounds like your problem, not mine."

Audrey looked back down at her lap and waited for him to leave.

"Where's the brush?"

She reached underneath her pillow and pulled it out. She was always careful with it so it'd be in the same condition as when he gave it to her. However, since he was overly suspicious, she never knew what he'd see that would cause his paranoia to kick in.

He inspected the brush before throwing it back on the mattress.

Now that he was gone, Audrey decided to do her exercises. Her routine had recently changed. Stretching had taken the place of sit-ups, and she didn't do as many jumping jacks and leg kicks now that her stomach had increased. With no need to rush, Audrey took anywhere from twenty to thirty minutes to complete her whole routine. It had become habit for her to repeat the process in the afternoon as well.

She drank the rest of her bottled water and resumed reading the chapter she started that morning.

About an hour after she finished reading, her kidnapper brought her food. The plate held her prenatal vitamin along with two plain waffles, scrambled eggs, and strawberries. He placed the plate and two bottles of water on the floor.

"Merry Christmas," Audrey whispered while staring at her lap. When she didn't get a response, she glanced his way.

The curious look he gave her made her nervous. *What's he thinking? Is he surprised I know what day it is?*

He turned and walked out of the room.

Her stomach had been growling ever since she woke up, so Audrey didn't hesitate to eat her breakfast. As she started in on the scrambled eggs, she reminisced about the breakfast she normally had on Christmas.

Her mother would make large, gooey cinnamon rolls, scrambled eggs, and bacon. Audrey always woke up to the delicious aroma permeating the house on Christmas morning. She smiled at the memory.

She didn't want to think about how much her parents must miss her, because it made life in this hell more miserable. Taking a large bite of one of the waffles, Audrey thought back on her first Christmas with Keith.

They had only been dating for three months. He had come over late that morning after opening presents with his family. Audrey's parents were still getting used to the idea of their daughter dating. They warmed up to him considerably when Keith brought over some homemade goodies he had helped his mother make.

Keith had always been a good guy, not just around her parents and friends, but also when the two of them were alone. Even their first sexual encounter had to be initiated by Audrey. She knew he didn't have the nerve to bring it up the topic.

Moving on to her next waffle, Audrey ripped off a small piece for her critter friends to devour later. Having enough in her stomach to take her vitamin, she twisted off the cap and drank half of the contents of the bottled water while swallowing her pill. She finished the strawberries and eggs and went back to the mattress to take a nap.

*Maybe I'll get something special today. It's Christmas after all.* She lay down and closed her eyes. *Wishing for anything good in this place is a bad idea. It only leads to more heartbreak.*

Waking up to the sound of the door opening hours later, Audrey looked over to see her captor coming in with a toilet seat in his hand. He placed it on top of the bucket then turned to her. "We're going outside. Put your shoes on."

After waiting for her to put her flip-flops on, he placed the blindfold over her eyes and escorted her outside. It had warmed up to around seventy degrees. The sun was shining on her, giving her a blanket of warmth as she walked alongside her kidnapper. After handcuffing her, he stomped off toward the fence where his horses were already waiting.

Audrey sat and watched as he fed and groomed his treasured pets. It had been years since she'd ridden a horse, but she wondered if her only means of escape might be riding one of those lovely beasts out of here.

When he was finished with the horses, the stranger came back to uncuff her and escort her back. As soon as they entered her room, she noticed the sheet and pillowcase had been replaced with clean ones. *The other kidnapper must've switched them out.* It had happened once before, shortly after her birthday.

Audrey guessed the other person was a woman. The clean sheets, somewhat nutritious meals, and "gifts" she received for her birthday, made her feel as though a female was showing kindness to her. It didn't make their part in her kidnapping any less criminal, but at least Audrey's time here had been made a minuscule less miserable. *No thanks to this guy*, she told herself as the stranger exited the room.

A few minutes later he returned with her dinner. The slices of carved turkey breast, mashed sweet potatoes, green beans, and buttered roll were accompanied with two more bottles of water. He didn't say a word as he laid the items on the floor and left her for the last time that day.

Sitting alone on the floor next to her Christmas dinner, Audrey felt a tear fall from her cheek. She placed her hand over her belly in time to feel her baby move.

"This is the last Christmas we're spending alone. Next year we'll be home with our family having a wonderful time," she whispered. She closed her eyes and prayed that was truly what the future held for them.

# Chapter 28

Darryl scanned the scene of a recent double homicide at a local convenience store. On New Year's Eve, shortly after midnight, both the owner of the store and one of his college-aged male employees were shot dead in the middle of the store. The shooter had gotten away, but the police were hopeful the security footage caught the culprit on tape.

It ate him inside that Darryl hadn't been able meet his Captain's deadline on locating a new lead in the Jennings's case. Telling her family and friends that he was being assigned to a new case had been even more difficult than he had imagined. Audrey's mother had sobbed when she heard the news, and her father shed a tear that he wiped away before his wife could see.

Keith's reaction wasn't surprising, but still tough to witness. Darryl allowed the young man to cry into his shoulder. Natalie, on the other hand, got angry, while at the same time she burst into tears. That was three months ago.

Darryl hated his job at times. How could he let that bastard, Aaron Smith, get away with this? *He's a slimy weasel who needs to be locked up.*

It was quarter to seven in the morning when his cell phone rang. "This is Detective Harris."

"Hey, it's Joe. Do you have a minute?" The officer asked with obvious excitement.

Walking away from the scene and toward his vehicle, Darryl replied, "Yes, of course. What's going on?"

"My department received word yesterday evening about a missing girl case out in Denver where police found the girl alive."

"That's great. But I'm guessing you're telling me this because it somehow relates to me?"

A short laugh came from the other end of the line. "Yes, that's what I'm getting to. The case was a fourteen-year-old girl who had gone missing due to a cyber pedophile. The creep had used a new type of spyware to monitor his victim and gain access to her computer files and Internet searches. The information he obtained he then used to make himself look like he shared her interests, thereby luring her out of her home to meet him. When the spyware was found on the girl's computer, police were able to link it to an IP address. This address was then used to locate the pedophile. That was how they were able to find the girl."

"I'm happy to hear the girl was found alive. Is there more?"

"Yes, the part you'll be ecstatic about. When I found out about the spyware last night, I realized it was possible your missing girl case from a few months back could've had the same spyware on it, given the timing of the two cases. I checked out Audrey Jennings's laptop from the evidence room this morning and did a quick search. You won't believe it. It was on her laptop!"

"You're telling me someone was spying on Audrey through her laptop?"

"You got it! The person on the other side of the spyware could see all her files, her Internet searches, everything. When I called the Denver police department to get more information on the spyware, they informed me it was so new they didn't know much about it yet. Fortunately, having just come across the program, they don't believe its creator is aware it's been discovered. That said, I was able to get the IP address of the computer that was spying on Audrey's laptop. I ran a search and have the owner's name for you."

Astounded by this new development in the Jennings's case, Darryl stared into the flashing red and blue lights of the cop cars scattered around the parking lot in front of him. "Joe, you're amazing! I'm wrapping up here and will be at the precinct shortly. If this leads us to the guy who kidnapped Audrey, then I owe you big time."

After hanging up, Darryl quickly searched for the bald CSI assigned to the current homicides. Darryl took down his findings before rushing off to the police station.

*Is it possible I now have the evidence I need to nail Aaron Smith for Audrey's disappearance? Is she alive after all these months?*

Rolling up to the precinct, Darryl practically sprinted to the IT department. He tapped twice on the door and was welcomed by Joe's smiling face.

"That didn't take you long."

"I was pretty much done processing the scene when I got your call. You said you had information on the IP address?"

Joe picked up the sheet of paper next to his keyboard and handed it to Darryl without breaking eye contact with him.

"Thanks again," Darryl said as he was halfway out the door.

He dropped into his desk chair and typed the name and address Joe provided. *Christian Atkinson of Boston, Massachusetts, who are you?*

Less than two minutes later, the results popped up. He read the report that detailed a Christian Atkinson of Boston, Massachusetts who graduated with a master's degree in information technology from the Illinois Institute of Technology. Christian had relocated to Boston shortly after earning his degree ten years ago. However, the results showed no current employer listed for him.

Darryl hit the print option and proceeded to the precinct's network printer to retrieve his printout. He read through the two pages of information on his new possible suspect, then located the phone number listed for Christian.

As he sat back in his chair, Darryl went back and forth for a few minutes wondering if he should share this new lead with Captain Reynolds or move forward with his own investigation until he had something more concrete.

Convinced he was making the right decision, he walked into his boss's office. "Captain, something has come up in the Audrey Jennings's abduction."

Forming his hands into a steeple in front of his face as his elbows rested on the arms of his chair, Captain Reynolds replied. "Go on."

Taking a seat, Darryl said, "Officer Brown recently discovered a new type of spyware on Audrey's laptop. This specific spyware was found on the computer of another missing girl case that was recently solved out in Colorado. Can you believe it?! Someone was watching Audrey before she disappeared. Officer Brown provided me with the name of the guy whose computer was on the other end of the spyware. Captain, this could be it—the lead we need to find the creep who took her."

Taking a minute to consider these facts as he spun his wedding ring around his finger, Captain Reynolds asked, "What do you plan to do next?"

"I want to fly up to Boston where this Christian Atkinson is and question him face-to-face. I know I don't have jurisdiction in Massachusetts, but if I contact the guy and spook him in any way, I may jeopardize this lead. It doesn't look like he's currently employed; therefore, he may not have reason to stick around if he feels threatened."

"Okay, but make sure you have a good address on this guy before you spend the time and precinct's resources on flying up there to question him. And I want you back here by Thursday morning, whether you've gotten anywhere with the lead or not. I'll put another detective on the convenience store homicides in the meantime."

After thanking his boss, Darryl returned to his desk to run a few more inquiries to verify Christian was truly at the address that pulled up in Darryl's original search.

He then purchased a ticket for the next flight to Boston. It happened to be leaving late tonight from the Melbourne Orlando International Airport. Finally, he booked a hotel room near the Boston airport. He decided he'd rent a car when he got there, if he even needed one.

Now that his accommodations were taken care of, he planned to head home early to pack and leave in time for his flight. But before he could do anything else, his work phone rang.

"This is Detective Harris."

"Hi, there. I'm calling to see if we're still on for lunch today," Mel's soft voice replied.

"I'm glad you called. I'm sorry, but I have to take a raincheck. There's been a new lead in the Jennings's case, and I'm flying out of Melbourne to Boston tonight to question a possible suspect."

"Wow, that's great news! I know how much that case has weighed on you. Do you need a ride to the airport? I get off at five o'clock today. I can swing by your place after that to pick you up."

"If you're sure you don't mind. I'd appreciate it."

"No problem. See you then."

Once he was off the phone, Darryl was back to his thoughts regarding Christian. *There must be something that'll help explain his connection to the case. Maybe his bank records or credit card statements will provide the details I need to link this guy to Audrey's half-brother.*

Darryl couldn't let go of his suspicions that Aaron Smith was involved in his sister's disappearance. *There's something about him—not just his egotistical, haughty mannerisms either.*

He hoped Christian Atkinson was the piece of the puzzle that brought his theory to light.

# Chapter 29

It was the first day of 2018. The light flickered on in the room, but Audrey had been awake lying on the mattress for the last hour.

Her kidnapper was getting more aggressive toward her by the day. There were times when she wasn't sure he would hold off on his plans for her until the baby was born, which was less than three months away.

A few days after Christmas, he had walked in on her doing her exercises and backhanded her. Even without a mirror, she knew there was a bruise on her face. She had thought, *What's so wrong with me doing exercises that he felt the need to hit me?*

Two days after that, she had left behind half of her meal—some beef stew she didn't want to eat with her hands. Hundreds of ants had come out to feast on it. Her kidnapper was irate. He had picked her up off the mattress and threw her up against the wall threatening to do more to her if she ever left food behind again.

The experience shook her. She could tell he was escalating, and there was no telling if he'd have the patience to wait a few months to kill her. At least that was what she assumed his plan was for her now that she had seen his face.

She sat up on the mattress and took a few swigs of her water before opening *Little Women* to the next chapter. It was her second time reading the book since her birthday. It had been difficult to limit herself to a couple of chapters in the morning and then another two in the afternoon after her nap. Especially on days when the stranger didn't take her outside.

Audrey couldn't figure out if he was busy with some sort of job on those days or if he considered it too cold for her to go out. Those days were exceptionally long. Having him come into the room at any moment as a loose cannon made things even more stressful.

The door crept open so Audrey set her book by her side.

In her kidnapper's hand was a plate holding two slices of whole wheat buttered toast, sliced ham, and a banana in its peel. As he set down her food and bottled waters, he said, "I'll be back to take you outside. Eat before I get back." Then he left her alone again.

Since she didn't know how long he'd be gone, Audrey slid off the mattress. She inspected the meat first and was thankful it wasn't lunch meat. It looked to have been cut from a spiral ham.

Audrey didn't know much about what a pregnant woman should or should not eat, but she once heard a friend's mom say she couldn't eat lunch meat unless it was heated up. It had something to do with the lunch meat possibly making the baby sick. Relieved she wouldn't have to leave it uneaten and face the wrath of her captor, she picked up a thick slice.

Her last shower was yesterday, where she was given another pair of sweatpants and a long-sleeved shirt to wear. They were on the baggy side, making it hard to do some of her exercises. While she was punished for doing exercises not long ago, there wasn't much else to do in this room to make the time go by. That, and she needed to keep up her strength in case she got the opportunity to outsmart or outrun her kidnapper. However, outrunning him might not be an option, given her ever-increasing pregnant belly.

After finishing the ham, she grabbed the banana. Taking a generous bite of the fruit, she thought of ways to escape. A thought that was on her mind day and night. It wasn't uncommon for her to wake in the middle of the night in a cold sweat, only to be reminded that her nightmare was her reality.

Opening one of the bottles of water, Audrey swallowed the prenatal vitamin with one large gulp. She rubbed her belly as her baby moved. It didn't take long in her pregnancy for her to realize the baby was most active after Audrey ate.

She allowed herself a few minutes to envision what it would be like if she were free from this place and able to deliver her baby with her family and friends there to support her. Images flashed in her mind of Keith's smile when his child was first put in his arms. The comforting hugs from her parents when they came to see her and their first grandchild shortly after she gave birth. And the loads of gifts her best friend would bring to spoil her honorary niece or nephew.

Audrey began to cry. Wiping the tears away with the sleeve of her shirt, she picked up the two pieces of wheat toast and the half-empty bottle of water.

Back on the mattress, she opened her book. Halfway through the next chapter, she pulled out her brush and worked it through the tangles that had developed during the night.

Feeling somewhat energetic, she got up and stretched while keeping an ear out for the locks on the door. Starting a new year with a black eye wasn't one of her resolutions.

A half hour later, she finished reading her second chapter, just in time for her captor to return.

He casually took a glimpse at the empty plate as he passed it. Audrey was tired of this routine but being chained in that lawn chair was the only way she got out of this room for any length of time. Due to the uncomfortable circumstances of her showers, Audrey tried to spend no more than five minutes on the whole process.

Outside, she instantly felt the brisk winter breeze hit her. It was only around fifty degrees out at almost noon.

After she was handcuffed and left alone in the chair with her blindfold off, she closed her eyes and lifted her face skyward to expose as much of her skin to the sun rays as possible. Despite the chill, she was grateful to be out of her lonely room.

Opening her eyes, she saw a small plane passing by. Taking a second to glance in the stranger's direction, she noticed he was busy brushing his horses. She sensed this might be her only chance at being rescued. Ignoring her fear, she attempted to make herself seen by rocking as far as she could from side to side. *Please, please, see me and send help!*

But sadly, the plane went by and didn't circle back around. Even worse, she looked in her kidnapper's direction again to see he was glaring at her.

*Oh my god! He must've seen me!*

He dropped the horse brush onto the ground and marched in her direction.

Her stomach did flips, and her heart started to beat faster. *He doesn't need much of an excuse to hit me so what'll he do to me for trying to signal for help?!*

When he got within arm's reach of her, he cocked his hand back and hit her across the face harder than he ever had. Audrey's vision went black and the ringing in her left ear was so intense she wasn't sure her hearing in that ear would ever be normal again. Then he swiftly uncuffed her from the chair and threw her backwards onto the ground.

Seeing the fury in his eyes, she knew he had lost all control. *He'll hurt the baby!*

Before Audrey could react, her captor kicked her left side hard with his work boot.

The jolt of pain made her scream. Out of sheer panic, she curled her body up to protect her stomach and yelled, "No, not the baby!"

Audrey remained in this curled-up position until he picked her up by her upper arms and yanked her to her feet. The pain in her left side was much worse with this sudden movement. She might have a broken rib, but all she could focus on was how the kick might've affected her baby. *Is he or she okay?! Do they feel the same pain I do?* Tears blurred her vision and before she could stop them, they began streaming down her cheeks.

Too distracted by what had happened, the kidnapper forgot to put her blindfold on. When they got to the building, he swung open the door.

Audrey could see the hallway she had walked through over a hundred times. It was built against a large barn. There was a side door and what appeared to be old windows with no glass all along the length of the hallway. She looked up into the openings as they passed by and saw there was a loft full of hay. All this time she thought she smelled something familiar as she came through here.

Realizing Audrey was taking in her surroundings, he stopped in his tracks and squeezed her arm even tighter. "Close your eyes!"

She immediately did as he said.

In the room, he threw her violently onto the mattress.

Landing harshly, her left side jolted, causing her to scream out from the pain.

The reaction angered him more and he smacked her across the face again.

Terrified of what he would do next, she instinctively curled her legs up in the fetal position like she had done outside. She tried not to make a sound but struggled to breathe due to the increasing pain in her side. Protecting her baby was more important to her than her pain.

Seconds later the door slammed shut.

The pain was excruciating, but Audrey carefully uncurled her body and stayed flat on her back. She used the air vent over the bed as a focal point while she steadied her breathing. She realized the next time she tried to escape she better be successful. Otherwise, there was no doubt in her mind he'd kill her.

While the thought terrified her, Audrey didn't have much time before her child made his or her way into the world. She decided her next attempt at escaping needed to be soon, very soon.

# Chapter 30

Sitting in his aisle seat on the plane headed for Boston, Darryl replayed the kiss from Mel over in his mind. She dropped him off at the airport, and before he climbed out of her Kia Sportage she leaned over and kissed him.

While it hadn't been their first kiss, it was *how* she kissed him that stuck in Darryl's mind. He wondered if the kiss was a sign that she was ready for the next step in their relationship.

He planned to get back to her as soon as he could to see if her feelings for him were as strong as his were for her. But before he could return to Florida, he needed to get Christian Atkinson to give up his accomplice. Darryl was convinced all roads in this case led to Aaron. *I just need to get Christian to confirm it.*

His nonstop flight landed three hours later at the Boston Logan International Airport at ten thirty at night. Since it was so late, Darryl decided to catch a cab to the hotel. With his carry-on in hand, he exited the airport to hail a taxi as he dialed Mel's number.

A thirty-degree wind blew through the terminal. He quickly used his free hand to pull the collar of his jacket up over his neck.

A taxi pulled up to the curb right in front of him so he hopped in the back seat and told the driver to take him to the Boston Marriott. In route, Darryl waited for Mel to answer his call. He was surprised at how eager he was to hear her voice.

"Hi, there, did you make it to Boston okay?"

*I'm falling hard for this woman.* Simply hearing her voice made him feel more alive. "Yep. I'm on my way to the hotel. My return flight is early Thursday morning, so I was wondering if you would like to go out to dinner and a movie Friday night? I thought we could catch up on my trip and see how your week went."

"Yes, I'd like that. How about I pick you up from the airport before I go to work on Thursday, and we'll iron out the details for Friday then?"

"Perfect."

As the taxi pulled up to the Marriott, Darryl and Mel said their good-byes.

After getting settled in his room, he ordered room service, showered, and changed into comfortable clothes.

Pulling out his laptop, he reviewed the results of his search on Christian's past. Darryl hadn't come across any large deposits into his bank account or found any odd charges on his credit card statements in the last year. *It's possible Christian was paid cash for his part in Audrey's disappearance.* Since there was no way to track a cash payment, Darryl had to use another strategy to coax a confession out of Christian.

A knock on his hotel door signaled his food had arrived. A good meal and a restful night's sleep were exactly what he needed to prepare for his visit with Christian.

The next morning, Darryl was up early. He poured his first cup of coffee and grabbed an everything bagel with cream cheese at the lobby buffet. Sitting at a small table in the corner of the large room, he pulled out the list of questions he put together for his newest suspect.

When Darryl had finished his bagel and coffee, he put on the heaviest coat he owned and left the hotel lobby. It was only in the forties outside so he quickly jumped into the back of a taxi waiting out front.

After giving the driver Christian's home address, Darryl sat back in the warm vehicle and watched from his side window as they drove by the snow-covered buildings and streets of Boston.

Twenty minutes later, the taxi parked in front of Christian's apartment complex. Darryl paid the driver, then crossed to the other side of the street to wait at the bus stop. If he attempted to go up to the suspect's apartment to confront him, Christian could deny talking with him and then the trip to Boston would've been a waste.

Wiping away an inch of snow from the bus stop bench with his coat sleeve, Darryl sat down and fished out the driver's license picture of his suspect from his back pocket. He stared at it for a minute before shoving his left hand into his pocket to keep it warm.

Glancing up and down the street, he noticed several instances of middle-class residents with their kids coming and going from the tall brick apartment buildings all around him. *Since today is New Year's Day, it's probably busier than usual out here.* A quick look at his watch told him it was just after eight.

An hour had passed, and Darryl needed to use a restroom and get inside somewhere to warm up. Looking around for a restaurant or convenience store in walking distance, he caught glimpse of a man exiting the apartment complex diagonal from him. While his hair was a bit longer and he now had facial stubble compared to his driver's license picture, he was definitely Christian Atkinson.

The suspect descended the flight of stairs and veered northbound on foot.

Darryl slowly rose from the bench and, as discreetly as possible, followed Christian from a distance on the other side of the road. Once Christian rounded the street corner, Darryl crossed the road, dodging mounds of gray snow piled up on the curbs. He practically jogged to catch up to his suspect who was now entering a small coffee shop.

*Thank God! I can use the restroom, get a cup of coffee, and interrogate this guy all in one place.* Darryl waited a minute to go into the coffee shop, so he didn't bring attention to himself. Then he stepped into the shop and casually let his eyes wander around the busy room. His eyes landed on Christian still in line waiting for his order to be taken. Darryl slipped into line behind the two folks that had entered the establishment right before him.

Christian had given the cashier his drink order before settling into a corner booth where he was tapping away on his cell phone.

Darryl quickly ordered his coffee and hurried off to use the restroom.

When he exited the men's room, Darryl heard the barista calling his name. He swung by the counter to collect his drink before making his move.

"Happy New Year, Christian. May I join you?" he asked with a big smile.

Christian gave him a penetrating stare. He was obviously trying to remember Darryl.

"Don't worry, you don't know me. My name is Detective Darryl Harris of the Cocoa Beach Police down in Florida. Your name came up during an investigation I'm working on involving a missing girl." He slid into the booth across from the now startled young man.

"I don't know anything about a missing girl. You have the wrong guy."

Darryl was certain, based on the guy's initial reaction to his statement, that he was very much the guy Darryl was looking for. "Yes, you are. You see, your computer was linked to spyware found on my missing girl's laptop. Now, you can tell me why you were spying on Audrey Jennings, or I can extradite you to Florida where you'll be forced to answer my questions."

The young man practically jumped when he said, "No, there's no need for that. I'll tell you what I know. But I have to say, I don't know what you're talking about. Are you saying someone is missing?"

"Yes, Audrey Jennings was reported missing back in August of this last year. She's been gone for five months, and the evidence points to you as our new prime suspect."

"I didn't kidnap anyone!" Then seeing the startled faces that turned to gape at him, Christian lowered his voice. "The spyware wasn't my idea. I did it for an old friend who asked for a favor. I had no idea the information on her laptop would be used to make her disappear."

While anxiously tapping his foot underneath the table, he continued, "He said a friend needed information. I figured it was someone who had a crush on her and wanted to find something he could relate to her on."

"What's the name of this friend who wanted the information?" Darryl asked, eager to hear "Aaron Smith" come out of Christian's mouth.

"I don't know the guy's name, but I can give you the name of *my* friend. I sent him all the data I found on her laptop. His name is Bill Nelson, and he lives in Rockledge down in Florida. Actually, I don't think he lives far from where you're from."

The look of realization on his face told Darryl he was putting two-and-two together.

"How do I know you're telling the truth? You could be sending me on a wild goose chase with this Bill Nelson."

"Do you have access to a computer to look him up?"

Darryl slowly nodded.

"Okay, then you can confirm Bill's information and see I'm not lying. We went to the same college—Northwestern University."

"I thought the search I ran on you indicated that you graduated from the Illinois Institute of Technology."

"Yes, that's true. But I started out at Northwestern. I changed majors when I decided not to pursue a career in law."

Darryl slid back out of the booth. "Okay, then let's go."

"Go where?"

"You're coming with me so I can verify what you're telling me is true. I'm not letting you out of my sight until then." He ushered a now sullen Christian out of the coffee shop to catch a taxi.

# Chapter 31

On the ride over to the hotel, Christian pulled out his cell phone. But before he could get past his password screen, Darryl snatched it out of his hands.

"Hey, what are you doing?"

"I can't take the risk you'll contact Bill Nelson, if he truly does exist."

Without an objection, but sporting an immature pout, Christian stared out the window opposite the detective.

Around eleven thirty, they arrived at the hotel and reached Darryl's room within minutes.

Darryl sat down in front of his laptop. *If things pan out with this Bill Nelson in Rockledge, then I may be heading back to Florida sooner than I thought.* When he noticed Christian hovering near the door, he said, "Come take a seat."

Darryl typed "Bill Nelson of Rockledge, Florida" and waited for the results. Glancing sideways at Christian, Darryl asked, "Why did you do something as criminal as loading spyware onto someone's computer, even for a friend?"

Christian squirmed in his seat. "Bill played baseball for Northwestern. And while he wasn't exactly popular, due to his size and strength on the field people respected

233

him. I, on the other hand, didn't fit in there. Let's just say Bill took me under his wing and made sure I wasn't a loner, like I'd been in high school."

"How did Bill know about the spyware? From what I've gathered it's fairly new."

"We kept in touch over the years and hung out for a weekend after the New Year last year. I must've gotten pretty wasted one night, because the next day Bill informed me I'd told him all about my project. I explained to him that I wanted to sell it to the government to be used against the dark web."

Darryl found it hard to believe the spyware was ever intended to be used for good. *So far, it has negatively affected the lives of two girls. At least two that I know of anyway.*

"When did Bill reach out to you for use of your spyware? Was it when he first found out about it or later?"

"It was later. I want to say sometime in mid-July. Bill said his friend was desperate for information about a certain girl. I guess I didn't know Bill as well as I thought."

Darryl sensed this part of Christian's story was genuine. "Some people are only what they want you to see them as. You'd be amazed at the descriptions I've gotten from family and friends of some of the worst predators I've arrested. They're so smooth they can create a whole other personality to trick people into not suspecting them of evil."

When Christian hadn't replied, Darryl continued, "How long was the spyware on Audrey's computer before you no longer had to provide information to Bill?"

"It was only about a week or two. I forwarded an Internet search Audrey had inquired about, and within a couple of hours Bill came back to me saying the guy found what he needed. I was a bit surprised, based on the search criteria she'd entered."

Darryl's eyes narrowed. "What was it she was looking for?"

"She was searching for adoption information."

Darryl wondered if this search had been the final straw for Aaron Smith. *If he thought Audrey knew about her adoption and would eventually start looking for her biological family, then Aaron could've been concerned about his wealth. No—correction—his and Audrey's wealth.*

The search results popped up on the screen as Darryl finished this thought. Scrolling through the details, he confirmed Christian was telling the truth about a Bill Nelson in Rockledge, Florida. "It looks as though this Bill has a degree in agriculture from Northwestern. However, his current employer is a veterinarian's office in Rockledge. That doesn't make much sense given his degree."

"Actually, I think he uses his degree more for his personal use than for his career. When I last saw him, I remember him telling me that he was working on his property—around fifteen acres, I believe. He planned to develop the land to make more room for his horses. He was really proud of them."

Darryl pulled up Bill's address on Google Maps and zoomed in on a small house in the middle of the property. It was located about thirty yards from what appeared to be a large barn. *Is that where Audrey was taken? Is it possible she's being kept there at this very moment?*

Turning to Christian, he said, "We're heading back to your place to pack a bag, then we're taking the next flight to Florida."

Christian's jaw dropped.

"You need to confess to your role in Audrey's disappearance, even if it wasn't intentional. And you also need to testify against Bill if it turns out he's involved. If you don't want to come willingly, then I'll have to get a warrant for your arrest. I'll give you one minute to decide if you're coming with me voluntarily, or if I need to take you kicking and screaming."

When Darryl promised Christian that he'd talk to the district attorney's office on his behalf, Christian hesitantly agreed to go to Florida.

Darryl called Captain Reynolds and filled him in on their plans. His boss then instructed Darryl to get back to Florida on the next available flight, while he put together the warrant to search Bill Nelson's property.

*I have every intention of being back in time for that search.* Darryl jumped back on his laptop to change his returning flight and purchase a one-way flight to Florida for Christian. To his relief, the next flight took off in less than three hours, and it had seats available. Darryl completed his purchase and packed his few belongings.

With his carryon-on slung over his shoulder, Darryl said, "Let's go. We don't have much time before our flight."

After stopping at Christian's apartment to allow him to pack a bag, they arrived at the airport less than two hours before takeoff.

Seated next to Darryl on the plane, Christian asked, "Do you think she's alive?"

Darryl looked up from the game he was playing on his phone. "I can only hope. Was there anything else about this mystery guy Bill mentioned? Any details you can think of could be helpful. Like maybe where they met or how they knew each other?"

"Nothing comes to mind. But now that you ask, he didn't talk much about his friend. It didn't seem odd at the time but thinking back I realize I should've asked more questions. I just saw it as my chance to help out a friend who had done so much for me."

The despair on Christian's face confirmed he had been used by his so-called friend.

*This Bill Nelson is a real piece of work.*

As soon as they landed in Melbourne, Darryl called Mel to let her know of his change in plans.

She answered her phone right before it went to voice mail. "Hi, is everything going well in Boston?"

"Actually, I'm back in Florida. There's been a huge break in the case, and I needed to take the next flight home. I'm going to get a rental car from the airport here and should be at the precinct within an hour."

"I'm glad to hear that. Let me know if you need anything, otherwise I'll see you tomorrow.

"You got it. I'm looking forward to it."

It was already six o'clock at night and dark out by the time Darryl and Christian loaded their bags into the rental car and took off for Cocoa Beach.

*Will we have to wait until tomorrow morning to search the Nelson property? If Audrey is alive, who knows how she's being treated.*

With so much running through his mind, Darryl didn't realize he was driving twenty miles over the speed limit. He quickly slowed down to a more reasonable speed and pressed the cruise control. He needed to get back to the precinct fast, but also in one piece. Otherwise, he'd be of no use to Audrey—assuming she was alive.

# Chapter 32

Audrey had remained still on the mattress with her eyes focused on the ceiling for the last two hours.

She finally mustered the courage to twist from side to side. Even though her left side would likely bruise badly from the kick, she didn't think she had any broken ribs.

Since the pain had subsided tremendously, Audrey gradually lifted herself up into a sitting position on the mattress and slowly stretched her arms up above her head. She could still feel the pain, but it was manageable now.

The physical abuse her kidnapper inflicted on her today was the last straw. Audrey decided it was time to do something. *If his ultimate plan is to kill me once my baby is born, then I don't have any other choice.* The fact that he'd think she was incapacitated from the kick to her side would be the advantage she'd use to catch him off guard.

He hadn't brought her food since that morning. So the next time he came through the door he'd almost certainly have a plate of food and a couple of water bottles in his hands. *That's when I'll make my move.*

Today was the day she planned to get out of this hell. She didn't know if she'd get another opportunity to escape the man who wanted her dead and intended to do who-knows-what to her child.

Preparing for her escape, Audrey did a few stretches on the floor while babying her left side. Even though she was convinced she didn't have a broken rib, soon she'd need to use whatever strength she had against her kidnapper. And her getaway would undoubtedly cause her side an enormous amount of pain.

Stopping momentarily to place her hand on her belly, Audrey felt the baby move. She whispered, "We're getting out of here soon, sweetheart. I'm going to do my best to get you to your father and grandparents. But if anything goes wrong, know that I love you more than I ever thought I could love someone." Fat tears dropped from her lashes. "You're going to need to be a fighter too, because we're in this together."

Audrey slowly rose from the floor and drank a couple of sips of water. Wiping away a tear, she took a few deep breaths to get her composure back. *He'll be here any time. I need to be ready.* Her heart was racing so she began walking laps around the room while inhaling some more deep breaths.

When she blew out her fifth breath, the locks on the door began to turn. *This is it!* Audrey quietly, but swiftly, went over to her makeshift toilet and lifted the seat off the bucket. Taking her place behind the door, she waited for him to enter.

As the door started to open, Audrey brought the toilet seat up over her left shoulder in the same stance as someone holding a baseball bat. When she saw her kidnapper's face come into view, she swung as hard as she could. The side of the seat nailed him directly at the bridge of his nose.

The surprise tactic worked. He fell hard to the ground, dropping the food and bottled waters he was holding.

Ignoring the piercing pain in her left side, Audrey jumped over his body as he reached for his nose. She scrambled into the hallway to the side door of the barn and pushed it open. To give herself a few extra seconds to get away, she closed it behind her. She hoped he'd assume she went out the other door at the end of the hallway.

Hearing him scream profanities, Audrey knew this was her only chance. *Now or never!* She couldn't go back—no matter what.

It was dark in the barn, making it hard for her to choose her next exit route. Her kidnapper continued to scream for her to come back. His voice was getting louder. *He's getting close!*

She ran to the other side of the barn. It was the side closest to the woods she had seen during one of her showers. After finding the sharpest thing she could use for protection—a small pair of pruning shears on a nearby shelf—Audrey reached the barn door. She pulled it sideways, just enough to get her body through. Closing the door behind, she took off in the closest thing to a sprint she could manage.

Audrey rushed for the wooded area only a few yards away. It was dark out so she struggled to see the stray tree branches she was running past. One whipped across her face, cutting her cheek and scarcely missing her eye.

She hesitated for only a second, because she could hear the barn door opening and her captor yelling for help from someone else. Gripping the shears she found in the barn, Audrey took off again. She had no intention of finding out who the other person was he was yelling for.

Less than twenty strides into her run, her foot caught on a small log. She stumbled but she quickly regained her balance. Her free hand reached for her abdomen, which was beginning to cramp. *There's no time to stop. I can't get caught or cramping will be the least of my worries.*

Deciding it best to cut across the woods to lose her captors, Audrey started running diagonally from her current path. She heard rushing waters nearby and headed in that direction. Her kidnapper was no longer yelling so it was hard to know how far behind her he was. If she stopped to listen for his footsteps, then she'd lose whatever head start she had gained from her surprise attack.

The glow of moonlight was the only thing allowing Audrey to see her surroundings. She hopped over a larger tree stump this time but didn't see the mound of dirt a few feet away from it. Suddenly, she was falling full force to the ground. She did her best to hit the ground without getting pierced by the shears, while simultaneously making sure she didn't land on her belly.

Hearing someone running behind her, she crawled behind a tree in hopes the person hadn't seen her. She could then run in the opposite direction when they passed.

Within seconds she heard footsteps on the other side of the tree. They stopped. *Can they see me?! Are they waiting for me to come out from behind here?*

Audrey tried to slow her breathing to make less noise as she sat paralyzed in fear.

The figure got closer, rounding the other side of the tree trunk where she was hiding. When the captor and his prey made eye contact, Audrey saw a burning rage in his eyes.

He closed in on her and bent to clutch her upper arms. Blood was dripping from his nose, and it already looked swollen. As he pulled her to a standing position, Audrey thrust the pruning shears into his left shoulder.

He immediately released his hold on her and tried to pull the shears from his body.

Audrey took off without looking back. The sound of rushing waters was getting even louder; she knew she was close. *If I can just get to it, there must be a way out of here.*

The cramping was getting worse. But she ran a bit farther and finally came up on an embankment. She peeked over the edge to see the river flowing down below. When Audrey was about to take another step for a closer look, she felt an arm reach around her. A needle was thrust into her neck. Everything went black.

***

Audrey started coming to with hazy vision. It was dark. Feeling the effects of the drugs wearing off, along with the exhaustion of trying to run away, she tried to reach for water.

Unable to move her arms, she looked down to see chains wrapped around her arms and legs. Her heart jumped wildly in her chest. And her head started to spin. The cramps she felt earlier were getting stronger. *What am I going to do?!*

It was clear things weren't going to end well for her. She'd have to beg her kidnapper to spare her child's life. Even if that meant she'd have to endure whatever punishment he gave her—including not making it out of here alive. With that thought, the light flickered on.

He walked into the room, closing the door behind him. This time he didn't have a plate of food or any bottled waters. Instead, there was a sharp knife in his hand, and an evil glare in his eyes. There was a significant cut where the toilet seat made contact with the bridge of his nose, and a dark bruise was already forming in between his eyes.

She frantically squirmed to free her arms and legs.

He meandered toward her, obviously relishing the fear the situation was creating in her.

As he got closer, she screamed, "*No, don't hurt the baby!*"

Ignoring her plea, he inched the knife upward so it was parallel with his torso before he covered the distance to the mattress. With a sinister smile, he unwrapped the heavy chains and started to yank down her sweatpants.

When she realized what he planned to do to her, she struggled to wiggle out of his hold. "*No! No! No! No!*"

Suddenly, the door burst open.

# Chapter 33

Darryl and Christian arrived at the police station at five minutes to seven that evening. Darryl rushed into the main room where Captain Reynolds and eight other officers were huddled around.

"Detective, you made it back in time. The officers and I are going over the plan for our search of the Nelson property. We're just waiting on the warrant. It took some time to persuade the DA's office that Bill Nelson was a man of interest in the Jennings's case, even with the information gained from Mr. Atkinson." Captain Reynolds pointed to the young man standing next to Darryl.

"How long do we think it'll take to get the warrant?"

"The assistant DA is trying to locate a judge to sign off on the warrant. It shouldn't be much longer. We have officers and K9s ready to head out as soon as we get the word. Why don't you get Christian comfortable in one of our interview rooms, and I'll have an officer in there shortly to take his confession."

Darryl nodded and led Christian out of the room.

When Darryl directed him to a chair, Christian anxiously asked, "You're going to speak to the DA's office on my behalf, right?"

"Yes, but you have to give the officer who comes in here the whole truth about what happened. Don't hold back any details. Plus, you're going to have to give up your spyware project. It was used not only in Audrey's disappearance, but in another missing girl's case. You'll also have to tell us everyone you sold or gave the spyware to. Everyone," Darryl repeated sternly.

"I understand. I never meant for anyone to get hurt." His legs started to bounce anxiously as he sat. "Whatever happened to the other missing girl?"

"I don't know all the details of the case, only that she was found alive."

The worry lines on Christian's forehead started to disappear. "None of this was supposed to happen. When I created the program, I thought it could be used for something good. But I needed money and choosing the right people to sell it to wasn't a priority at the time."

It sounded like the truth, but Darryl found it difficult to feel sorry for the guy whose project affected the lives of two girls so terribly—possibly even ended the lives of one of them and her unborn child. "You can't go back in time and fix what you did. However, you can be honest with us now and give up the names of the people who have your spyware."

An officer knocked twice on the door before entering. The veteran officer was holding a legal pad and pen and wore a stern expression.

Darryl and the officer exchanged a quick nod.

"Okay, Christian. The officer will take your confession now. I'll be leaving with the others to search Bill's property and bring him in for questioning. When I get back to the precinct, I'll speak to the DA's office and let them know you've been fully cooperating with the investigation."

When Darryl left the interview room and saw the officers in the main room were still waiting around, he took a sharp turn into the kitchen for a much-needed cup of coffee. Since his nerves were getting the best of him, eating wasn't even a thought.

Taking a sip of his coffee, he decided to keep himself occupied by checking his voice messages. The first message was from Mr. Jennings. This didn't surprise Darryl. Audrey's father had called to check in at least once a week since Audrey disappeared.

"Detective Harris, this is Daniel Jennings. I'm calling to see if you've heard anything new in my daughter's case. That's all. Please give me a call back when you can."

It always brought Darryl a jolt of heartache to get these messages. Not only from Audrey's parents but from her best friend and boyfriend.

The second message was from Mel. "Just making sure you made it there safe. I've been assigned to go tonight to the Nelson property to gather evidence. It looks like I'll see you sooner than we planned. Talk to you soon."

Taking another sip of his coffee, Darryl gave her a call back.

Mel answered, "Hey, how are you?"

"I'm okay. We're still waiting on the warrant. Which reminds me, please be careful tonight. I know you won't be the first one on the scene, but we don't know what this guy is capable of."

"I will, but you be careful too."

They ended their short call with good-byes.

A war waged within Darryl's subconscious. *Do I call Mr. Jennings back and notify him of this new development, or do I wait until we've searched the Nelson property?* Every minute Audrey's parents didn't have news about their daughter had to be hell, but Darryl didn't want to give them false hope either. *Maybe a few hours of false hope are better than nothing.* And with that last thought, he dialed their number.

"Hello," Mrs. Jennings answered somberly.

"Mrs. Jennings, it's Detective Harris. Is Mr. Jennings there?"

"Yes, I'll go get him from the other room."

"You can put me on speaker. I have some news for the two of you."

"We're both here," Mr. Jennings replied.

"We've come across a new lead in your daughter's case. There's a possible suspect. At this point we're waiting on a warrant so we can search his property. I'll contact you once I know more."

"What can we do? Should we come down to the police station?" Mr. Jennings asked excitedly.

"No, you both should stay home. If you want to do something, then pray. Pray we come back with more than just news."

"Thank you. No matter what you find, we appreciate all you've done to help locate our daughter," Mrs. Jennings choked out before she left the call.

Mr. Jennings added his thanks and hung up.

Darryl hoped he hadn't set them up for epic disappointment. *We need that warrant soon if we're going to search the property tonight.* He hated the thought of having to wait until morning. It was already seven thirty and he could feel his impatience getting the best of him. He crossed the room to his boss's office.

"Hey, Captain."

"I haven't heard anything yet, but it shouldn't be much longer."

"Right. I wanted to let you know that Mr. Jennings left me a voice message earlier today. I called the couple back and told them we're working on a lead."

His boss's eyebrows turned upward.

"They've waited months for some news—for anything that could give them hope their daughter would be found."

"You're not worried you're giving them false hope by telling them we have a lead—even one as promising as this one?"

Darryl started to chew on the inside of his cheek as he sat. "Maybe. But if it were your daughter, wouldn't you want even a few hours of hope to break up the months of despair and helplessness?"

After a short pause, Captain Reynolds replied, "Yes, I guess I would. Be careful though. They must be in a fragile state by now. Whatever we find at the property, I sincerely hope they can take the news," he sat forward in his chair, "and you can as well."

Darryl looked curiously at his boss. Then the comment clicked. He had taken the Cocoa Beach Killer case so personally it had cost him his marriage. While that case had stretched over a longer period than this one, there was no guarantee he was going to get a better outcome. "Is there a way to do this job well and not put every part of yourself into it?"

Captain Reynolds half smiled and reclined in his seat again. "I suppose not. But I hate to see you go down the same road as before. Seems like you have something good going with Ms. Crosby. Try not to screw it up."

Even though he knew this statement was more of a joke than a serious comment, Darryl replied, "I don't plan to." He gave Captain Reynolds a smirk before going back to his desk.

Since he knew his boss had already discussed the details of the Nelson property with the officers earlier that evening, Darryl pulled up the address one more time on Google Maps.

He took note of how close the barn was to the small house. He also noticed that there looked to be an extension built on to the side of the barn. *It doesn't look like it's made of wood. Maybe it's a large concrete tack room, seeing as Bill owns horses. He could be storing saddles in it if it's air conditioned, since it's too humid to keep them out in the elements.*

After zooming in on the property, Darryl spotted a large concrete slab next to the barn's extension. *What's that for?* But before he could examine the image on the screen any longer, he heard Captain Reynolds yell. "We got it! The warrant has been signed! Let's hit the road!"

The officers that were dispersed around the main room of the precinct immediately hurried toward their vehicles parked out front.

Captain Reynolds rushed out of his office. "Darryl, wait up. I'm riding with you."

"Yes, sir," Darryl responded, as they jogged out of the building to find their missing girl.

# Chapter 34

Darryl drove up to the Rockledge property at twenty minutes after eight. There wasn't much light except for what was coming from the windows of the small house.

The house wasn't much bigger than one thousand square feet and needed both cosmetic and non-cosmetic repairs. Its blue paint had aged and was peeling in multiple spots around the exterior. There was wood rot all along the bottom third of the house, and the roof had seen better days, with patch work in different areas throughout.

Darryl and his boss were the first to arrive at the scene. They had parked at the end of the driveway, so they wouldn't alert anyone inside the house of their presence. Their plan involved a surprise tactic in case Audrey was alive and this was the only way of keeping her that way.

As they climbed out of the vehicle, the other four cop cars from the Cocoa Beach precinct pulled up behind them. The Rockledge Police Department had been notified of the search but were only on standby if needed.

Pulling the document from his jacket, Captain Reynolds handed it to the officer who was standing closest to him. "Officer Kentz, here's the warrant. Go ahead to the house and notify Mr. Nelson of the search. And take two other officers with you. I'm going to have the rest of the officers leave the K9s behind for now and go to the back of the house in case he tries to escape. Detective Harris and I are going to search the barn to see if anyone is in there."

The officer took the warrant. "Yes, sir."

Captain Reynolds and Darryl cautiously passed the house and drew their 9mm guns as they came up on the barn. Darryl started to slide the large barn door open. As it rolled aside, they heard a woman scream, *"No, don't hurt the baby!"*

Running in the direction of the scream, they could hardly make out the door to the side of the barn through the darkness. With weapons still drawn, Captain Reynolds carefully opened it so Darryl could proceed through it first.

It was even darker inside the hallway. Darryl glanced to his left to see a door at the end of the hallway. Then he automatically looked to his right to see another door with light streaming from under it. *Audrey must be in there.*

Captain Reynolds followed him but held back as Darryl swung open the door and hollered, "Police!" He immediately caught sight of Audrey lying on the bed with her assailant at her legs.

The suspect leaped up from Audrey's lower half to hold a knife to her throat. "Get back or I'll kill her!"

"You don't have to do this, Bill," Darryl calmly said. "The girl is alive; that's all that matters. We can all walk away from this. But if you do anything to her, then I don't have any choice but to shoot you."

"You're going to get out of our way, or I'll slice her throat!" He yanked Audrey from the bed as he stood and placed her body in front of his, all the while keeping the knife to her neck.

Audrey had tears streaming down her face as her fear-filled eyes fixated on Darryl.

Darryl noticed Bill appeared to be in tremendous pain. His face contorted every time he moved. *Has he been injured? His left arm is hanging limp to his side.*

A glimpse at Audrey's abdomen confirmed Darryl's suspicions that she was pregnant. His attention immediately went back to the assailant. "How about I put my gun away and you let her go. I won't come after you."

"You're going to put your gun away, and Audrey is coming with me. Otherwise, I'll end both their lives." Bill looked down at Audrey's abdomen and back up at the detective.

"Fine, you win."

Bill eyed him suspiciously. "I don't believe you. You're going to put the gun on the ground and walk out of here. Then we're going to follow behind you. If I see you move even an inch for your gun, the girl dies."

Audrey whimpered as the knife grazed her throat.

Darryl slowly set his weapon on the floor and kicked it away, so it wasn't easily accessible to Bill either. He then raised his hands in a show of surrender. "The gun is gone. I'm going to walk out of the room now." Moving backwards out of the doorway, Darryl didn't see his captain anywhere in his peripheral view. *Where'd he go?*

He took his time walking down the hallway so as not to make any unintentional, sudden moves. When he got to the end of the hallway, Darryl backed into the door that led to the outside. "I'm going to open the door now, so we can all exit without anyone getting hurt."

Bill didn't respond, so Darryl reached around and twisted the handle. He backed out of the narrow space, raised his hands over his head again, and turned to stand a few feet behind the open door.

When Bill and Audrey got around the door, there were six officers waiting for them with their weapons drawn. The panic on Bill's face disappeared as quickly as it had appeared and was replaced with fury.

"Bill, you have nowhere to go. You need to release Audrey," Darryl said.

Bill looked around at the firearms aimed at him.

Darryl saw Captain Reynolds come into view from around the corner of the barn. He snuck up behind Bill and placed a gun to the back of his head. "Let go of the girl, or I'll blow your head off."

Before Darryl could register the expression on Bill's face, the suspect pulled back the knife as a sign he was going to use it on Audrey.

Darryl yelled, "*No!*" as an officer shot at Bill—just inches from Audrey.

The sound of the gun shot terrified her, and Audrey instinctively dropped to the ground.

Bill was momentarily stunned by the bullet that grazed the same arm that had the injured shoulder. He launched toward his victim to use her again as his human shield.

But before he could reach her, two other officers shot him directly in the chest. He staggered backwards until his body hit the ground.

Captain Reynolds got down on one knee to check Bill's vitals, while Darryl rushed to Audrey's side. "Are you okay?" Quickly looking her over, Darryl didn't see any obvious injuries other than a scratch on her cheek.

"Yes, but I think I'm having contractions. They started as cramps earlier when I tried to get away. But now the pain has gotten much worse," she said in between deep breaths.

Darryl glanced at Captain Reynolds, who was shaking his head to confirm Bill was dead. *Shit! How are we going to prove Aaron was involved in Audrey's disappearance?* Since he didn't have time to dwell on that, Darryl picked Audrey up and carried her to his car.

Having just arrived at the scene, Mel jumped out of the CSI van and ran up to Darryl. "Is that Audrey?!"

"Sure is. She thinks she's having contractions. I need to get her to the hospital right away." Darryl carefully set Audrey in his back seat.

"I'm coming with you." And without waiting for an objection, Mel ran around the vehicle and got into the back seat next to Audrey.

Captain Reynolds caught up to them at this point.

"Captain, I'm taking her to the hospital. Can you call Audrey's parents and let them know to meet us there?"

"You got it. I'll catch a ride back to the precinct with another officer. Get her to the hospital safely."

Darryl dropped into the driver's seat and simultaneously buckled his seat belt as he started the car and put it in reverse. "How are you doing, Audrey? Are the contractions coming closer together?"

Her eyes were squeezed shut. She was holding her breath, but she took the time to respond. "I'm not sure."

Seeing that Audrey couldn't track her contractions in the state she was in, Mel cut in. "I'll time them for you, Audrey. Just let me know when the next one starts. Okay?"

Audrey gave her a quick nod as she exhaled.

When Audrey was in between contractions, Darryl asked, "How far along are you?"

Bashfully, Audrey looked in his direction. "I'm six and a half months pregnant." Agony took over her features as she confirmed, "I'm having another one."

Mel started to time it with her watch. A minute later the pain had subsided enough for Audrey to open her eyes.

"Okay, let me know when the next one begins."

Darryl took the opportunity to interact with her again. "Audrey, do you know who kidnapped you?"

"No, I don't think so. I saw him at the mall about a week before he took me. He was staring at me so intensely I thought it strange at the time. But otherwise, I have no idea who he is."

"Was there anyone else involved in your kidnapping? Anyone you saw or heard your captor talk about?"

Audrey's face scrunched up, and she wrapped her arms around her abdomen.

Mel looked at her watch and said, "They're only three minutes apart. You need to get us to the hospital fast. The doctors need to stop her contractions before she delivers this child too early."

Glancing at his GPS screen, Darryl could see they were five miles away from the nearest hospital. Increasing his speed, he prayed he'd get there in enough time. Otherwise, her parents would be showing up to the hospital to find out about a deceased grandchild.

# Chapter 35

Darryl sped up to the front entrance of the hospital as two nurses came running out with a gurney. Thankfully, Captain Reynolds had alerted the hospital of Audrey's condition and when to expect her.

Darryl jumped out of his car as one of the nurses opened the car door closest to Audrey. The male nurse gently lifted Audrey up onto the gurney with Darryl's assistance.

When the nurses pushed Audrey through the lobby doors, Mel walked around the vehicle and joined Darryl as he leaned back against his car. Exhaling their relief, the couple stared into the hospital's automatic glass doors.

"No matter what happens in there, you never gave up on that girl. And she's no longer in danger of being harmed by her kidnappers."

"But what if I didn't find her in time to save her child?"

Mel got up from her position against the car to stand in front of Darryl. "You did all you could. Beating yourself up over what happens next doesn't help anyone. You're a great detective. The fate of that child is in God's hands."

She leaned in and kissed him gently on the lips.

He pulled her close and kissed her more passionately than he ever had. They stayed in this position, enjoying the feel of being in each other's arms, when they were suddenly brought back to reality. Keith ran past them into the hospital.

Recognizing him instantly, Darryl shouted, "Hey, Keith! Wait up!"

The young man slowed his pace. When he turned to see who was calling him, he abruptly stopped.

Darryl and Mel quickly caught up to him in time to wrap their arms around him as he began to weep.

"She's okay. It's all okay," Darryl said. Though he wasn't a hundred percent sure it was the truth.

"Mr. Jennings called me after he got off the phone with your boss. He said Audrey is alive and being taken to this hospital. Her parents will be here any minute. She's really okay? And her kidnapper is dead?"

"She's alive. And her kidnapper was shot. He passed away at the scene. But I think I should tell you something before you get up there. Audrey's six and a half months pregnant and having early contractions."

Keith stared at the couple while he processed this information. "The baby might be in trouble? Where's Audrey? I have to be with her." He started racing toward the front desk again.

Darryl and Mel followed closely behind him.

The clerk at the desk pulled up Audrey's name in her computer and notified them that she had been admitted to the labor and delivery unit on the third floor. "You'll have to go up to that floor to see which room she's in."

Practically running to the elevators, Keith hit the button and impatiently waited for a door to open.

"Hold it together. Audrey's going to need you to be strong—for her and the baby," Darryl instructed.

Keith nodded.

When an elevator door eventually opened in front of them, they all started loading into it. As the door began to close, someone hollered, "Hold the elevator!"

Keith threw out his right arm to stop the doors and stepped out halfway to wait for the familiar voice.

Mr. and Mrs. Jennings jogged to the elevators. Mr. Jennings wrapped his arms around Keith and then waited for his wife as she did the same. Stepped onto the elevator, they were clearly happy to see Darryl waiting in it with a beautiful woman.

"Detective, it's so good to see you!" Mrs. Jennings said as she gave him a bear hug. She had been crying, but Darryl sensed they had been tears of joy.

Mr. Jennings shook the detective's hand emphatically. "We can't thank you enough for finding our daughter. Captain Reynolds told us you're the one responsible for following the lead that resulted in Audrey's rescue."

"I'm just glad we found her. That's all the thanks I need."

The doors opened to the third floor. As they exited the elevator, Darryl said, "I'll go ask for Audrey's room number. Keith, why don't you sit and talk to Mr. and Mrs. Jennings about their daughter's condition." He gave the young man a meaningful look.

Keith slowly nodded. "Sure," he replied hesitantly.

As Darryl and Mel walked away, they heard Mrs. Jennings. "What condition? What's wrong with Audrey?" There was a shake in the dear woman's voice.

At the check-in desk, Darryl said, "I'm Detective Harris. I'm looking for the room number of a patient who was brought in earlier. Her name is Audrey Jennings. She's about six months pregnant and having contractions."

The woman gave him an inquiring look, so Darryl showed her his badge. It did the trick. She began typing. "Ms. Jennings was taken to room 315. I'll call you when she's in stable condition and able to see visitors."

"I appreciate that. Thank you."

Mel took a minute to observe the three individuals talking at a small table on the other side of the room. She turned back to Darryl. "Let me get you a cup of coffee from the cafeteria downstairs. I think the three of them need some time to discuss things, and it might be a while before the doctors determine the best treatment for Audrey."

Darryl also watched the discussion taking place between Audrey's parents and Keith. The couple was hugging him and crying. Since it didn't look like things were getting heated between Keith and the Jennings, Darryl took Mel up on her offer.

In the elevator, Darryl took a glimpse at his watch: 9:37. It had been a productive twenty-four hours. Feeling the effects of not eating since that morning in Boston, he wondered if there was anything left in the cafeteria to eat.

At the first floor, the elevator doors opened to reveal an anxious Natalie Anderson. "Ms. Anderson, it's good to see you," Darryl said with a smile.

Too impatient and emotional to stop and talk to him, Natalie immediately jumped into the elevator as they got off it. She hit the button for the third floor, but before the doors closed, she flashed him a small smile. With tears ready to fall from her eyes, she said, "Thank you for finding her."

*Wow! A thank you from the best friend. Miracles really do happen.* His smile widened.

He and Mel located the cafeteria to find it had already closed for the day. A janitor cleaning the floors directed them to the vending machines down the hall. To both their relief, there was a coffee vending machine amongst the snack ones.

Mel slipped her credit card into the machine and bought a cup of regular coffee for Darryl and a hazelnut cappuccino for herself.

With his coffee cup in hand, Darryl scanned the contents of the snack machines. "Are you hungry? I'm going to get a bag of pretzels for myself."

"Yes, I'll have the same, please."

They took a seat in the first-floor lobby. Opening their bags of pretzels, the couple sat in silence drinking their caffeinated beverages and munching on their snacks. The only noise was coming from the evening news on the lobby television.

"Want to come back to my place tonight?" Mel asked him an hour later. He looked over at her, and reading his stunned reaction wrong, she added, "After we know Audrey's condition is stable, of course."

He began to laugh. It was a good feeling after all the tension he had built up that day. "I would love that."

When the pretzels and coffee had been consumed and the news had switched to a late-night talk show, Mel and Darryl headed back up to Labor and Delivery. Getting off the elevator, they noticed the sitting room was empty.

Darryl approached the desk. "I see our friends are no longer up here. They may have already gone in to see Ms. Jennings. I believe you said she's in room 315."

This time the clerk responded right away. "Yes, Ms. Jennings can see visitors now. You can go through the doors to the right."

Darryl took Mel's hand in his as they strolled through the doors the receptionist indicated.

They came to a wall of signs with room numbers and arrows. "Room 315 is to the right," Mel pointed out.

Down the hallway they saw the door to room 315 was ajar. Hearing soft voices inside, Darryl gently tapped on the door.

"Come in," Mrs. Jennings welcomed.

Darryl pushed the door open and signaled for Mel to enter before him. Inside the room, they saw Keith sitting up against the bed railing to Audrey's left, holding her hand, while Mrs. Jennings was on the other side holding onto the bed rail. Mr. Jennings was sitting in a chair in front of the hospital bed.

"You must be feeling better. I guess the doctors were able to get your labor to stop," Darryl said as he smiled at his newest rescue.

Audrey gave him a smile in return. "Yes, they gave me an IV of something called Terbutaline, which slowed down the labor pretty fast. They said it should be enough to hold off the labor until the baby is ready to come on his own."

With a sneaky smile on her face, Mel asked, "*His?*"

The family members, along with Natalie, started to laugh.

"Audrey, I don't think I formally introduced you to my girlfriend, Mel Crosby. She's a crime scene investigator who was instrumental in your case."

Audrey turned to Mel and said, "Thank you for all you did to help find me. And good catch. They did an ultrasound when I was first admitted, to make sure the baby is developing on schedule. The doctor said the baby is not only healthy, but that we're having a boy." Audrey was beaming as she gazed adoringly at Keith.

He returned the sentiment with a kiss to her hand.

"Congratulations. That's wonderful news," Darryl said. "Did the doctors say when you can leave the hospital?"

Rubbing her protruding belly, Audrey answered, "As long as labor doesn't start up again in the next twenty-four hours, they've assured me I can go home by tomorrow night. Thankfully, the kick to my side didn't result in any broken ribs."

Darryl felt a wave of relief now that Audrey and her baby were in stable condition. He then took down all the details Audrey could remember of her kidnapping. Thirty minutes later he and Mel said their good-byes and drove to her place.

This time, however, he wouldn't leave her in the morning like a coward.

# Chapter 36

Strolling through the hospital doors around nine o'clock the next morning, Darryl was carrying a dozen assorted donuts and a cup of coffee.

On the way to Mel's apartment the night before, he had called his boss to get an update on the other kidnapper. Captain Reynolds assured him there was no need to go to the precinct after leaving the hospital. Ever since they arrested Gina Johnson, Bill's longtime girlfriend, she'd only mourned Bill's death and wouldn't speak a word to any of the officers.

*A night in a jail cell may get her to open up.*

Darryl decided to check on Audrey before going to the police station to interrogate Ms. Johnson. He got off at the third floor and saw the same woman from the prior night at the desk.

She automatically buzzed him through the doors to the labor and delivery unit. As he passed by, he held up the box of donuts. She smiled but shook her head.

Down the hall, he spotted Audrey's door was closed. He wondered if it was too early to check on her. Thinking about how early it was reminded him of who he left behind in bed that morning. Being an early bird, he was up around seven, even though he and Mel hadn't gotten to sleep until well past one o'clock in the morning.

However, he hadn't acted like an idiot this time. Before leaving her apartment, Darryl had kissed Mel good-bye and promised to have lunch with her later that day. To his relief, Mel had assured him she understood.

*How can I be so lucky to be with such a smart, beautiful, understanding woman?* Darryl grinned before tapping on Audrey's door. If she wasn't awake, he figured he'd leave the donuts for the nurses working that unit.

A small voice answered. "Come on in."

Darryl opened the door with one hand while carefully balancing his coffee on the donut box in his other hand.

Audrey was sitting up in her bed, while Mrs. Jennings was passed out on the pullout bed in the adjacent corner of the room.

Audrey smiled at the detective as she waved him in.

"I'm not disturbing you too early in the morning, am I?"

"Not at all. After all the sleep I got in that lonely room all those months, I can't seem to sleep more than a couple of hours at a time now. It's as though if I sleep for too long, the nightmare will come back. I know it's silly, because if I wake up this time my nightmare will actually go away."

Darryl could see her eyes were moistening with tears.

"Thank you for rescuing me. If you hadn't shown up when you did, I truly believe he would've done something horrible to me." She dabbed at the tears with a tissue she had pulled from a box beside her bed.

He gave her covered knee a small squeeze. "From what I've heard about Bill's wounds when they brought him in for the autopsy, you inflicted some major pain on him before I showed up. Keith said you were a fighter, and I have to agree with him. It took a strong person to endure what you went through and still fight back."

Mrs. Jennings started to stir. Rubbing her eyelids, she said, "I'm so sorry. Have I been asleep long?" She directed her question to her daughter.

"No, not long enough. I don't think you got but an hour of sleep. Seriously, Mom, you should go home and get some rest."

"Keith said he'll be by with breakfast around nine and will stay with you while I go home to shower."

Audrey turned to Darryl. "It took me agreeing to my mom staying overnight, for the guys to go home and get some sleep. They all came up with a plan so I wouldn't be left alone."

Mrs. Jennings slowly got up from the pullout bed and shuffled over to give her daughter a hug. "There's nothing wrong with us wanting to be with you every minute of the day. We've been deprived of being with you for too long." Her voice cracked with emotion.

273

To lighten the mood, Darryl interrupted, "Well, it probably doesn't compare to what Keith is bringing you for breakfast, but I have donuts if you're hungry."

Audrey's eyes widened. She signaled for him to bring the box closer. "They look amazing! I haven't had a donut in forever. Thank you." She chose a Boston crème and took a large bite out of it right away.

He waved the box in Mrs. Jennings's direction. It did the trick because she walked over and scanned the assortment. Choosing a simple glazed donut, she thanked him and found the seat closest to her daughter.

Seeing the mother and daughter enjoying their donuts, Darryl turned to Audrey. "Well, I have a suspect to interrogate so I better get going. If you need anything from me, or if you remember something outside of what you told me last night, don't hesitate to call me. I'll check back in with you before you get released today."

The women thanked him again for the donuts before he set the box on a nearby table and took off.

When he stepped off the elevator into the lobby, he saw Keith practically running through the main hospital doors with two large brown paper bags in his arms. "Whoa, whoa, where's the fire?" Darryl joked as he held the elevator door open.

"Thank you. I ordered Audrey's favorite breakfast, chicken and waffles, but the restaurant lost the order. Then they took forever to get it for me when I got there."

"Don't worry. Audrey's safe and sound in her room. All is good." Darryl was thankful he could say that. It didn't appear that way twenty-four hours ago.

Up in Audrey's room, Keith finally arrived with breakfast. After a kiss from his girlfriend, he started unloading the contents of the two bags he brought. He placed the Styrofoam container of chicken and waffles onto the rolling table in front of Audrey's pregnant belly. Then he pulled out a set of plastic silverware and a couple of packets of butter and syrup from the other bag.

"My favorite! Thank you," Audrey said and gave Keith another kiss.

"How's everyone doing this morning?" Mr. Jennings greeted as he ambled into the room.

"You weren't supposed to be here for another hour," Mrs. Jennings said warmly.

"Yes, well, this is where the party is, so I couldn't stay away." He looked over at Audrey and gave her his signature Dad wink.

"Yep, the party is definitely in here," Audrey said, then she glanced down and added, "and you're stuck with this crazy crew. Maybe later in life you'll wish I had chosen adoption for you." Audrey chuckled as she rubbed her belly affectionately.

Mr. and Mrs. Jennings exchanged a concerned look.

"I think it's time," Mrs. Jennings said to her husband. He nodded.

They took a seat near the hospital bed, moving their chairs closer to each other. "Audrey, we need to tell you something," her mother began.

Audrey took their change in mood the wrong way. "I'm not giving up my baby if that's where you're going with this. It was something I thought about when I first found out, but it didn't take me long to realize I couldn't live without him."

Keith looked at her when she said this, but he didn't say a word.

"No, dear. Of course not. That's not what we need to tell you. There's something about your past we didn't want you to know. But after what happened to you, we feel the need to be completely honest with you. No matter what you decide," Mrs. Jennings managed to get out.

Audrey's focus moved from one parent to the other. "You're starting to scare me. What is it?"

Seeing his wife struggle to get the words out, Mr. Jennings picked up where his wife left off. "Audrey, you know you mean the world to us, and nothing about what I'm about to tell you changes the fact that you're our daughter. And we love you more than our own lives."

Audrey nodded with creased brow.

"Sweetie, your mother and I adopted you right after you were born. Your biological father had died, and your biological mother was young and living in a women's shelter when she was pregnant with you."

Giving her time to register this astronomical news, Mr. and Mrs. Jennings sat in silence. They held hands and waited for the first question to come.

Audrey finally asked, "Adopted? You're saying you're not my biological parents? Why? Why are you telling me this now?"

Mr. Jennings explained, "Audrey, it's possible one of your blood relatives is searching for you. During the investigation into your kidnapping, a witness disclosed they had seen a man with similar features as you at one of your volleyball matches."

Audrey didn't say anything right away. Taking time to process this, she looked at her hands in her lap and then at each of her parents. "I think I need some time to myself."

Mr. Jennings could see his wife was struggling to keep her emotions in check. He replied to Audrey, "Honey, how about Keith stays here with you, and Mom and I will go home now. We can call you when we're heading back to the hospital."

Audrey answered with a short nod.

"It's okay. I'm not leaving," Keith spoke up.

Mr. and Mrs. Jennings each gave Audrey a hug and hesitantly slipped out of the room.

# Chapter 37

Arriving at the police station at quarter to ten, Darryl made a beeline for Captain Reynolds's office. After knocking on the doorway, he waited for his boss to look over from his computer screen.

"Come on in."

"Cathy at the front desk said Ms. Johnson has been escorted to interrogation room two. Has she given up any information since being brought in?"

"No, nothing. She just keeps crying about her boyfriend. Unfortunately, she'll be a hard one to crack. I know your suspicions regarding Audrey's half-brother. Good luck getting her to give him up."

Darryl stopped by his desk to collect a pad of paper and pen. Seated in front of his computer monitor, he took a few minutes to think through his line of questioning. If Gina Johnson wasn't willing to speak to the police, then he needed to use a different tactic than the other officers.

Going over the details Audrey had provided him late last night, he tried to figure out what role Gina Johnson played in the kidnapping. There had to be a reason why someone, who had no criminal record, allowed a pregnant woman to be held against her will by their boyfriend. *This might be my hardest interrogation in this case yet.*

Confident he had come up with the right strategy to start his interrogation, Darryl veered toward the interrogation room. He walked in to see a woman with her face buried in her arms. "Good morning Ms. Johnson, I'm Detective Harris."

Her head popped up from the table with a scowl on her face. "Are you the cop who killed Bill?"

"No, I didn't shoot your boyfriend. However, he was shot because he was going to stab Audrey Jennings."

"He'd never do that to—" She suddenly stopped shouting.

"He'd never do that to whom?"

She leaned back in her chair and crossed her arms over her chest. Her unruly red curly hair looked to be as unmanageable as her attitude was at this very moment.

*I need to go in another direction to get her to talk.*

"Ms. Johnson, you don't seem like the type of person who kidnaps pregnant girls and keeps them locked in a room. My guess is it was your boyfriend's idea to keep Audrey locked up until she gave birth. Then he planned to rape and kill her."

"That's not true! The plan wasn't to kill her!"

He paused to consider her reply. "What was the plan then? If Bill wasn't going to kill her, then why'd he kidnap her?"

Gina glared at him.

"Did the officers tell you Bill tried to rape Audrey right before we found him and Audrey in that room?"

Her eyes went wild. "You're lying! That's not possible! He despised that bitch! He couldn't wait for the baby to be born so we didn't have to deal with her anymore."

When she didn't say anything else, he prodded her even more. "Or was he waiting for the baby to be born so he could have his way with her when she wasn't pregnant?"

This question did the trick. She lost all control of her emotions. "That's not true! He loved me! He did it all for me! That's why he took her—because I wanted a baby!"

*Finally, the truth! That's why she was involved.*

Now Darryl needed her to give up Aaron Smith as the man behind the kidnapping. "You're saying you and Bill kidnapped Audrey for her baby? But why her? There had to be plenty of pregnant women to kidnap who were further along in their pregnancies."

With a cynical laugh she replied. "You don't get it. Bill didn't go looking for a pregnant girl to kidnap. The baby was offered to him by someone related. Don't you see? That baby would've been better off with us."

*There it is! My confirmation. Now I have that bastard!* Needing her to say his name, Darryl continued his interrogation. "What you're telling me is it wasn't Bill's idea to kidnap Audrey, but someone else's? Do you remember this family member's name?"

Gina looked baffled. "I don't remember his name, and I never actually met him. Bill had known him for years though. Kidnapping Audrey was a way for them to help each other out."

"Do you happen to have a phone number for this mystery man, or maybe an address?"

"No. They mostly talked in person."

Darryl was suddenly taken back by this remark. It seemed odd, since Aaron worked and lived in Chicago, and Bill worked and lived in Rockledge, Florida. Then again, Aaron was down to see Audrey at her volleyball match. *Maybe Aaron was lying about how often he visits the area.*

"Ms. Johnson, things don't look good for you at this point. Your boyfriend is dead, and you'll be charged as an accomplice in Audrey's kidnapping and attempted murder."

Her head whipped up to meet his gaze. "He wouldn't have needed to kill her if she didn't remove her blindfold! It was her fault! She was supposed to have the baby and be returned home, where no one would know who took her."

*Returned home? That can't be true.* "Are you saying this relative didn't want her dead? Wasn't that the original plan?"

Her eyebrows turned down, and her eyes narrowed. "No. It wasn't until she saw Bill's face that it was decided she couldn't go back. According to what Bill told me, the guy was extremely upset about it. He threatened to call the cops until Bill explained to him that the kidnapping had been his idea and he'd go to jail too."

Darryl jotted down these details.

She added, "The ironic part is Bill did everything he could to keep our identities secret so Audrey could go back home without anyone finding out who took her. He even wiped away any evidence from her personal items left behind at the church."

*This doesn't make sense. Why would Aaron want Audrey returned to her family after the baby was born?* "You said Audrey's disappearance was a way for Bill and this guy to help each other out. If the baby was for you, then what did Audrey's relative get out of the deal?"

"*Her* relative?" Gina asked, then she began to laugh bitterly. "You don't get it, do you? I'm not saying another word until you can guarantee I won't be charged for any part of the kidnapping."

Darryl couldn't believe what he was hearing. *Does she really have information or is she bluffing?*

"Stay here, Ms. Johnson. Let me see what I can do." But when he left the interrogation room, he notified the officer waiting outside the door that he could return her to her jail cell. And instead of going to the DA's office,

Darryl headed to the Nelson property to see if he could find out what Gina wasn't willing to tell him without a deal.

# Chapter 38

Darryl looked around the property. There were two Cocoa Beach cop cars, a Brevard County sheriff's vehicle, and to his pleasant surprise, the CSI van parked in the driveway in front of him.

Mel's boss had retrieved the van from the property late last night and drove it back to the ME's office. *Mel must be back working the case.*

He smiled and nodded at a couple of officers on his way to the house. Climbing the squeaky wood steps that led to the front door, Darryl could see the police tape across the door had been loosened. Pulling on a pair of latex gloves, he turned the doorknob and ducked under the tape as he stepped inside.

There was a small, well-kept kitchen off to the right as he entered the house. He heard a drawer being shut somewhere inside the house. "Hello, Detective Harris here."

A smiling Mel rounded the corner, coming from a room down the hallway to his left. "I was wondering if I was going to see you before lunch."

"That's right. We may need to reschedule for another day," he said, giving her a kiss. "Have you found anything suspicious since you got here?"

She led him back down the hallway to a bedroom. "I haven't been here long. After doing a quick walk-through, I decided to start back here in what looks like the couple's bedroom. I'm guessing you didn't get much from the girlfriend, since you're here so soon."

"You're mostly correct. She didn't give up Aaron Smith like I was hoping. However, she did say the original plan was to return Audrey back to her parents once she gave birth. Oh, and she and Bill were going to keep her baby."

"Return her to her parents, but keep her baby? Why not just kill her if they were going to take away her child?" Mel shook her head in disgust.

"Supposedly it wasn't until Audrey saw Bill's face that the plan changed. I'm not sure if I believe her story though. There was something she was cryptic about. Anyway, I was hoping to find what she wasn't willing to tell me."

"Then I'll let you get to work. If you need anything just let me know."

He leaned in to give her another quick kiss.

Since Mel was starting her process in the bedroom, Darryl proceeded into the living room and began by looking at the framed pictures displayed in the TV entertainment stand.

The photos were of Bill and Gina over the years. Some were of the two of them alone or with different family members and friends. *They look happy. How'd they get to the point of kidnapping and attempted murder?*

After searching the living room, he moved on to the kitchen. Darryl opened each of the drawers and cabinets but found the usual kitchen utensils and cooking accessories. There was a pantry near the bay window, but it contained only food and baking supplies.

When he closed the pantry door and turned around, he spotted a small two-drawer metal file cabinet underneath the kitchen counter that faced the bay window. *Strange place for a file cabinet—but then again, it's a small house.*

He opened the first drawer, but there was nothing but phone chargers, extension cords, and an old PlayStation gaming system in it.

The second drawer, however, was filled with file folders full of papers. The folders were labeled and in alphabetical order by the type of paperwork they contained. There was one for "Bank," another for "Car," and so forth.

Darryl fanned through a few more file folders until he got to one labeled "Legal." He removed the folder from the cabinet and started flipping through its contents: adoption paperwork and foster care applications. The adoption paperwork hadn't been filled out, but it included a retainer fee of fifteen thousand dollars in bold letters on the top of the first page. It was dated eleven months ago.

*That's a hefty amount of money for a couple who lives in a home that needs major work.* But as his eyes roamed the inside of the house, he could tell the couple kept a tidy home, despite the condition of the outside.

Returning his attention to the folder in his hands, the next document he came across was a rejection letter from a foster-care organization. It was a more recent document, dated nine months ago. Darryl did a quick calculation in his head. *Only five months before Audrey was kidnapped.* The letter listed the reasons they were denied. The first reason was that they weren't married, and the second was due to the condition of their home.

*So, they couldn't afford to adopt a child, and they didn't meet the requirements to foster a child. No wonder they became willing participants in this scheme.* Darryl wondered why the couple wasn't married, since it was part of the reason they couldn't foster a child in this county. He pulled out his cell phone and searched for the contact he wanted.

"Hi, Darryl. What's going on?"

"Hey, Joe. Have you finished running the background check on Gina Johnson for the Jennings's case?"

"Sure have. And I placed a copy of the search results on your desk."

Not wanting to leave the Nelson property quite yet, Darryl replied, "I know she doesn't have a criminal record, based on a quick search I ran before her interrogation. But did you see anything in your search that explains why Ms. Johnson and Bill Nelson weren't married?"

"Why weren't they married? That's an easy one. Because Gina Johnson is still married to a guy named Nathan Johnson. According to the divorce paperwork that was filed over five years ago, the process was held up. She and her husband share a substantial amount of debt."

Darryl continued to comb through the file folders in the drawer as he listened.

Joe continued, "The divorce documents state she denied knowing anything about the credit cards her husband allegedly opened in both their names and about being a co-signer on two of their cars. Whether Gina was lying or not, the couple couldn't come to an agreement in mediation and the divorce was never finalized."

"I wonder why they didn't file for bankruptcy and get a divorce after that," Darryl said out loud.

"Well, Ms. Johnson owes quite a bit in student loan debt, which is the only debt that currently can't be forgiven in bankruptcy court," Joe provided.

At the mention of this, Darryl came across a file folder labeled "Student Loans." He pulled it out and flipped it open to find receipts for payments Ms. Johnson had made over the last five years. According to a consolidated loan statement dated a month ago, she currently owed over thirty thousand dollars.

*That's it then. Gina couldn't afford to pay for an adoption, because she's trying to pay off her student loan debt so she can file bankruptcy and divorce her husband. At the rate she's paying off these loans, it'll take her another seven or eight years.*

"Ms. Johnson started out with a lot of debt for someone living in a home in need of major repair. What did she get a degree in?"

"That's the thing. I wondered the same, so I pulled up her college transcript. But Gina never finished college. She flunked out of nursing school in her final year. Worse, she barely makes over minimum wage working in retail."

"Thanks, Joe. I need to do some more digging, but as always, you've been a great help."

After getting off the phone, Darryl scanned the remaining files to see if anything else stood out. When he didn't find anything indicating a link between the couple and Aaron Smith, he walked down the hallway to the bedroom where Mel was working.

She was not only looking for potential evidence for this case, but for evidence of any other crimes the couple may have committed. There was always the possibility Audrey wasn't their first victim. Darryl doubted it, given the information he had recently found, but they had to do their due diligence.

When he stepped into the room, Mel asked, "Did you find anything good?"

"Kind of. I understand somewhat why the couple was willing to be a part of this kidnapping. I found a file containing both adoption and foster-care paperwork. In their specific situation, it didn't look like either option was going to work for them."

"They must've wanted a child badly to do what they did. It doesn't excuse what they did, of course. A young woman almost lost her life."

Darryl nodded and walked over to the bedroom closet. "Have you gone through here yet?"

"No, I was going to search in there next. Go ahead."

He nodded and started pulling out the three medium-sized boxes sitting on the floor next to the couple's shoes. Aside from the boxes and shoes, the only other items in the closet were the clothing up on hangers and a few old board games up on the top shelf.

When Darryl opened the first box, he found it filled with stuffed animals. They didn't look new, so he assumed they were either Gina's or Bill's when they were younger.

The second box contained winter clothing—some hats, scarves, and gloves. When he got into the third box, Darryl saw a pile of old baseball cards, a few medical textbooks, and two photo albums.

Darryl flipped through the purple photo album first. There were pictures of a younger-looking Gina and possibly her ex, if Darryl were to guess. Some pictures were of Gina with what looked to be her girlfriends and maybe even her parents.

Grabbing the black album next, Darryl opened it to reveal the first photo: Bill's high school graduation picture. He skimmed through the rest of the album, but there weren't many photos of family and friends. There were more pictures of horses and old vehicles than of people.

As Darryl got to the last page of pictures, he froze. *It can't be.* He pulled the photo from its clear plastic pocket and stared at it in complete shock.

Thoughts, events, and conversations were whirling in his head. *It's not possible!* "That lying son of a bitch!" he yelled out loud, not able to hold back his contempt for the guy.

He snatched his cell phone as Mel jumped up from the floor on the other side of the room and was at his side in seconds. "What is it?"

Before he could explain, someone picked up on the other end of the line. "This is Detective Harris. Connect me to Audrey Jennings's room 315 right away. It's an emergency."

Mel stared at him wide-eyed, realizing he had discovered something big—very, very big.

He put the phone on speaker while he waited to be connected. "Sorry, sir. Ms. Jennings was released and left the hospital a few minutes ago."

"She wasn't supposed to be released until later today. Who was with her when she left?" he asked, knowing her cell phone was in the evidence room at the station. When the person on the other end answered, he instantly replied, "Shit!"

He immediately hung up the phone.

Mel asked, "What's going on?"

"Come with me. I'll explain on the way. I have to get to Audrey before he's able to do something else to her or the baby," Darryl said as they ran out the front door.

# Chapter 39

Darryl and Mel fastened their seat belts as Darryl jammed the key into the ignition and put the car in reverse.

"What did you find in there?" she asked, completely stumped by his reaction on the phone.

He handed her the photo, and it took her only a second to recognize the two men. "No, it can't be! How?"

Speeding onto the main road toward the hospital, Darryl replied. "I was so convinced it was Aaron who planned Audrey's kidnapping that I've been totally blind to the real mastermind."

"The bastard fooled everyone. So, what's the plan?"

"Audrey doesn't have her cell phone with her; therefore, I'll need to track her location based on who she's with." He glanced sideways to see if she got his meaning.

Her eyes met his, and she nodded.

Darryl chose Captain Reynolds's number on his dashboard monitor. Two rings later his boss answered.

"Captain, I know who's behind Audrey's kidnapping. The person whose idea it was, I mean. I'll explain later, but right now I need to find Audrey. She left the hospital with her boyfriend a few minutes ago. She doesn't have a cell phone, so I need the GPS coordinates of her boyfriend's phone."

"Why not just call her boyfriend and ask him where they're at?" his Captain asked, confused.

"Because Keith was the one who planned her kidnapping."

Captain Reynolds took a moment to reply. "You have evidence to back this up?"

"I sure do."

"Okay. I'll get that information and will send it to your cell phone. I'll also have two officers meet you at the location for assistance. Be careful."

When he got off the phone, Darryl increased his speed.

"How are you going to confront him? With Audrey there, I mean?"

"I haven't gotten that far yet. It makes sense now. Gina said when Audrey saw Bill's face, and they told Keith that they'd have to kill her, Keith threatened to call the police. Something tells me he believes he loves Audrey, but the baby was a factor he didn't want to deal with."

Mel looked back at the road as she gave this some thought. "You're saying he loves her enough to want to marry her someday, but he doesn't want their baby?"

"There must've been a good enough reason in his mind for what he did. I just have to get him to confess to whatever that reason is. And I have to do it while getting Audrey safely away from him." His cell phone vibrated. "They're at Audrey's house, which means we have to not only get Audrey safely away from him, but her parents too. The officers Captain Reynolds promised better get there fast because we're only ten minutes away."

Those ten minutes passed in a blur, and before they knew it, Darryl and Mel were sitting outside the Jennings's residence waiting for the officers to show up. "I need you to stay out here when the officers arrive."

"No, I can help. Tell me what to do," Mel replied.

"It might be too dangerous. I don't want something bad to happen to you."

"You have three innocent lives in there," she said as she pointed to the house. "If anything happens to any one of them, and I don't at least try to help, I won't be able to live with myself."

He smiled at her and leaned in for a kiss. "Okay, but if Keith tries to get away or draws a weapon, I want you to get out of there as fast as you can."

The cop car they were expecting pulled up behind them. Darryl got out of his car and approached the vehicle. After speaking with the driver, he returned to his car. "Okay, they're going to park down the road so they can come up on the house unseen after we go in. One officer will be positioned at the front door and the other will cover the back in case Keith tries to run, or worse, take a hostage."

Mel trailed Darryl to the front door.

When he got a nod from Mel that she was ready, Darryl rang the doorbell. He knew it was important to act casual until they knew where Keith was in the house.

Mrs. Jennings answered the door. "Detective, Ms. Crosby, it's good to see you both. Come on in."

Darryl managed a smile as he and Mel stepped into the house. "It's our pleasure. I called the hospital and they said Audrey had already been released. Is she here?"

"Yes, Keith's helping her get settled in her room. Her father and I told her about the adoption. It hit her hard. She asked us to give her some time before she's ready to talk about how she feels and ask us questions. I can go get her for you though. I'm sure she'll be happy to see you."

"No need. How about you and Mr. Jennings go outside with Mel for a bit."

Her brow creased, but Mrs. Jennings did as the detective said. "Daniel, let's go outside for a bit," she called into the next room.

Mr. Jennings joined them in the hallway. "Hi, there. How are you folks doing?"

"Honey, we're going to visit with Ms. Crosby outside. I believe Detective Harris wants a private word with

Audrey." She turned her attention to Darryl to see if she had this correct.

"Yes, that'll be great. It shouldn't take long," Darryl replied with the same phony smile as earlier.

Once the three of them had left the house, Darryl hurried to Audrey's room. He tapped on her door and heard a female's voice answer. "Come in."

Cautiously walking into the room, he could see Audrey sitting up in her bed with Keith sitting at the end of the bed near her feet. The bed was in the far-right corner of the room as he entered.

"Detective Harris, it's nice to see you. Checking in on me again?" Audrey asked with a bright smile.

"You got it. I heard you left the hospital earlier than planned. You and the baby must be doing well," he said, while trying to figure out a way to create distance between the couple on the bed.

"Yes, the baby and I are doing great. Thanks to you. I really can't thank you enough for rescuing me."

Taking a quick glance over at Keith, Darryl noticed the uneasiness in the guy's expression.

"I'm glad everything worked out. Even though Bill was killed at the scene, I was able to question his girlfriend earlier today." He looked back at Keith. The young man's fingers were fidgeting with the comforter at both his sides.

"A girlfriend. That explains a lot," Audrey said out loud to herself.

"What's that?" Darryl asked.

"There were certain things that I knew, or he outright told me, were not Bill's ideas. Such as a cupcake for my birthday, along with a book to read and a brush for my hair. And the bed sheet was changed a couple of times while I was there. What did his girlfriend say? Did she explain why they kidnapped me?"

Keith wiped away a bead of sweat from his forehead. It was cool in the house, so this had to be his nerves working overtime.

Darryl lowered himself into the desk chair on the other side of the room. He was only five or six feet away, but he didn't know if he'd need to get up in a hurry. So, he decided to lean forward in the chair to lessen the distance—just in case.

"Actually, she did provide me with some helpful information. She said the plan to kidnap you didn't involve killing you until you saw Bill's face. They wanted your baby, or at least the girlfriend did. If you couldn't identify them, they had planned to return you home."

Audrey gasped. "They were going to keep my baby and send me home like that would make everything okay?" She began to tear up.

Based on the guilty expression on Keith's face, Darryl suspected it wouldn't be much longer before the young man said something or made a move.

"Keith, I'm sure you're happy to have Audrey back home, safe and sound. And in plenty of time before the baby comes. Your parents must be excited to know they're going to be grandparents soon."

Wiping away a tear, Audrey said, "You didn't tell me what your parents said about the baby. I know my rescue was on the news because I saw it on TV last night. But they didn't reveal my pregnancy. Did you tell your parents?"

"No."

"Why?"

When Keith didn't respond, Darryl felt the tension thickening in the room. "Audrey, how about I have a word with Keith, man to man."

Before she could answer, Keith finally chimed in with a voice thick with irritation. "That's okay, detective. It's apparent you're itching to tell Audrey the truth."

Unsure of what was going on in Keith's head, Darryl decided to tread lightly. "The truth? You must be talking about this." Darryl reached into his jacket pocket and pulled out the picture he had found at the Nelson house. He got up and handed it to Audrey.

She stared at it. Then the significance of it became clear to her. It was a picture of a group of young baseball players and their two coaches. What stood out was that one of the players was her boyfriend and one of the coaches was Bill Nelson, her kidnapper. She slowly looked over at Keith with betrayal in her eyes.

The guilt had finally gotten the best of him. "I knew you might be pregnant. The night of the Fourth of July party the condom broke, but I was afraid to tell you. I knew you would want to keep the baby, and I wouldn't be able to convince you to abort it."

Audrey's mouth hung open. When she didn't deny this fact, Keith continued. "When I went to baseball camp the week after the party, Bill was there. He was my coach for the fourth year in a row, and we had stayed in contact over the years. On the first day of camp, Bill could tell something was bothering me. I needed to tell someone so I confided in him. By the end of camp, he told me he knew someone who might be able to help me with my situation."

"What did you do? How did you know for sure I was pregnant?" Audrey asked with raised voice.

Keith didn't answer, so Darryl jumped back into the conversation. "Audrey, Bill Nelson had a friend place spyware on your computer. When you searched for adoption in late July, it confirmed Keith's worst fears. Isn't that right, Keith?"

Keith gave him a murderous glare.

Audrey looked at her boyfriend, then at the detective, and then back at Keith. "That can't be true. Keith?" When he didn't respond, she continued her frantic questions. "You had me spied on because you were afraid I was pregnant? Then what?!"

Keith didn't say a word as he moved his gaze down to his lap.

Darryl replied, "He and his friend Bill came up with the plan to kidnap you. Then, once the baby was born, you'd be returned home, and everything would go back to normal. Isn't that right, Keith?"

Tears spilled onto Audrey's cheeks. "What were you thinking?! As if I could move on with my life without my child. Never knowing who had him or how they were treating him."

Keith finally faced Audrey. "I wasn't thinking! I panicked! I had plans! *We* had plans! We were supposed to go to college, have a good time, get a degree, then come back here and *eventually* get married and have kids. My parents would have disowned me if they found out I got you pregnant before we were married. And I would've lost my chances at owning the family business."

Darryl may have assumed the wrong man was behind Audrey's kidnapping, but he guessed right when it came to motive. *It almost always comes down to money.*

"Did you know they were going to kill me?"

Keith's focus was back on his lap. "I begged Bill not to hurt you. I told him that there had to be another way. But he said he and Gina had too much to lose, and there was no way of getting around it. I even threatened to go to the police. The plan was never for you to get hurt. I thought I knew Bill better than that."

Audrey slid out of the bed.

Darryl cautiously rose from his chair, ready for whatever move Keith might make.

She let her tears flow freely as she shouted, "You bastard! I never want to see you again! I hope you rot in prison for the hell you put me and my parents through!" Audrey stormed past Darryl and out of her room.

"It's time you came with me, Keith," Darryl said as he inched his way to the door.

The anger the young man displayed moments ago was replaced with shame—and possibly heartbreak.

Keith slowly stood as Darryl approached him. "Keith, you are under arrest for the kidnapping of Audrey Jennings. You have the right to remain silent. Anything you say, can and will be used against you in a court of law." As Darryl gave Keith his Miranda rights, he cuffed the young man's wrists behind his back.

When they made it out to the front porch, Darryl saw a hysterical Audrey being embraced by both her parents. The looks of disgust they directed at Keith left no doubt they knew the truth about him.

Darryl escorted the young man to the cop car that was now parked in front of the house. When Keith was settled in the back seat, Darryl said, "You had everything going for you. But the truth is, you never deserved Audrey *or* your baby."

And with that said, the detective shut the car door and walked away.

# Epilogue

*March 2018*

Two and a half months later, Darryl moseyed into the hospital and passed the lobby desk to the elevators. He knew exactly where he was going.

Getting off on the third floor, he proceeded to the receptionist desk at the labor and delivery unit. "I'm here to see Audrey Jennings. Her son was born earlier today." He beamed with pride.

The woman looked up Audrey's room number and kindly told Darryl, "Yes, she's in room 324." She then buzzed him through the security doors.

Darryl was ecstatic to meet the little boy who shared his first name. Audrey decided to thank the detective for all he had done for her, and her son, by naming him Darryl Daniel Jennings. Her father was also honored that his first grandchild would have his name as his middle name.

Peeking around the corner into her room, Darryl could see there were already people visiting the new mom. Mr. and Mrs. Jennings sat on the small couch in the corner with smiles on their faces. Natalie was standing by Audrey's bed rocking the sleeping newborn in her arms.

Then there was Mel, who had arrived before him because her shift ended an hour ago.

Darryl walked over and gave Mel a gentle kiss.

She was sporting the engagement ring Darryl gave her a week ago when he proposed to her at dinner at a riverside restaurant. She said yes—after making him wait for what felt like an eternity on one knee in front of the whole restaurant.

"Detective Harris, so glad you could make it," Audrey said with a wide smile.

Turning his attention to Audrey, he said, "I didn't want to miss meeting the little guy."

Everyone looked over at the slumbering child.

Darryl said, "Your parents told me you'll be attending college in the fall. Still going to Gainesville?"

Natalie handed the now-awake infant over to his mother.

Audrey replied, "No, I've decided to go to a closer college. I got accepted to Stetson University, where Natalie is going. We both start in the fall."

"Stetson, that's great! Are you going to play volleyball there?"

Laying her son against her chest, she answered, "No, I won't have time for school, volleyball, and this little one. So, I'll go to class during the day and my parents will watch Darryl while I'm gone. And thanks to you, I don't have to worry about having a scholarship to attend such an expensive college." She winked at him.

Darryl smirked as he recalled providing a copy of Jeremy Smith's last will and testament—along with Audrey's DNA results—to Audrey and her parents. It didn't take long for the lawyer Mr. and Mrs. Jennings hired to reach out to Aaron and his lawyers and get a trust fund set up for Audrey. She'd never have to worry about money for her or her son.

It might not be enough to pay back what Jeremy Smith did to her biological mother, but since Audrey was the result of his attack, something positive resulted from it. And now a second positive factor: her son.

Audrey had spoken to her biological mother over the phone quite a few times since learning she was adopted. And even though the news had hit her hard, Audrey eventually forgave her parents. She admitted that she never doubted their love for her, and that they had raised her like their own blood.

She had asked her parents if they'd be okay with her having a relationship with Marissa.

It had taken some time for Mr. and Mrs. Jennings to become comfortable with the idea of Marissa being in their daughter's life. But when they found out Audrey's biological mother didn't want any part of the money that her daughter had received from her half-brother—even after Audrey had offered it to her—the couple's hearts were softened toward the new relationship.

Darryl was thrilled to see the smile on Audrey's face as she gazed at her baby.

It was only three weeks ago that Darryl learned Keith Lennox wouldn't be going to trial. Audrey's ex confessed to his part in her kidnapping and was planning to plead guilty to the charges against him. He made a deal with the DA's office to serve no more than twenty years in jail. Only seventeen of those years would be served if he displayed good behavior during his confinement.

Audrey had expressed mixed feelings about the outcome. She was thankful that Keith signed away his rights to his son. But she also confessed that she planned on telling her son about his father someday—when he was much older.

Forty-five minutes later, Darryl and Mel said their good-byes and left the hospital room.

When they got off the elevator and strolled through the hospital lobby, Darryl's cell phone rang. "Hey, Captain. What's up?"

"Darryl, I know you just got off a short while ago, but I have some news."

"What's going on?"

"The body of a young woman was discovered at the beach. There's reason to believe that the Cocoa Beach Killer is involved."

Darryl stopped in his tracks outside the doors of the hospital.

Mel gave him a concerned look, to which he responded, "They think the serial killer is back."